ABOUT THE AUTHOR

JOSEPH WEISBERG was born and raised in
Chicago and now lives in New York City.
He wrote his first short story, "The Mid-
Life Crisis Exploits," when he was twelve.
10th Grade is his first novel.

10th Grade

10th Grade

a novel

JOSEPH WEISBERG

RANDOM HOUSE TRADE PAPERBACKS • NEW YORK

2003 Random House Trade Paperback Edition

Library of Congress Cataloging-in-Publication Data
Weisberg, Joseph.
10th grade : a novel / Joseph Weisberg.
p. cm.
ISBN 0-8129-6662-7
1. Teenage boys—Fiction. 2. High school students—Fiction.
I. Title: Tenth grade. II. Title.
PS3623.E45 A615 2002
813'.6—dc21

Random House website address: www.atrandom.com
Printed in the United States of America
6 7 8 9
Book design by Jessica Shatan

To Mom and Dad,
For so much encouragement,
And to my classmates:
I still dream about you

**Come on Angel
My heart's on fire**

—Rod Stewart

10TH GRADE

By Jeremiah Reskin

DEDICATION

To my Mother and my Father

THIS IS NOT MY ACTUAL FAMILY

CHAPTER 1

THE END OF SUMMER

I'm starting right before the beginning. That way you'll get to know some of the main characters like my parents and my 2 sisters even though they're not really the main main characters. Anyway I don't know if you've ever been on a camping trip in a National Park or anyplace like that so let me describe The Grand Teton National Park in Wyoming where it's the end of summer. Believe me it gets very very dark there darker than in Hutch Falls or wherever you live because there aren't any houses with lights and stuff and you're surrounded by all the stars they're talking about when they talk about there being billions of stars. And craters in the moon. Also the moon gets really low when you're out there almost like it's right over your head.

So picture this it's a night like that but even darker it's so dark we can see everything up there but not much down on the ground except our tents which were in our basement non-stop for about 2 years since the last time we used them and are glowing the color orange now because of the lanterns inside. So we can see them. And the tents are glowing and I swear it looks like we're just floating out in the middle of space right in the middle of all the stars and planets and other stuff out there which in a sort of cosmic way I guess we are.

All the main characters in my family are here including my Dad my Mom and Claire and Beth (my 2 sisters). My Mom and Claire and Beth are inside 1 of the tents they're whispering then laughing then sort of laugh-whispering you can see them moving from outside like shapes. My Dad's with me by the campfire which by the way is burned out and he keeps getting up and walking around he's wearing what he wears camping which is this blue mesh undershirt he thinks is the greatest undershirt ever yellow shorts black socks pulled up high and this is the worst a pair of old black dress shoes he used to wear to work.

"It's alright" he says and he goes over to our car which is a station wagon which is parked a few feet away. The station wagon is yellow and it's about 10 years old my Dad bought it 2 years before from my Uncle Henry who was selling it because no one in the world would want it because it was such an old yellow piece of crap except my Dad. He walks around the car looking at it like he's checking it out like he did when he was thinking about buying it from Uncle Henry because if you ask me he had no idea how to look under the hood or check the engine or anything like that then he comes back to the fire.

"It's OK it's natural. Women" he says.

He comes back over to me.

"Women it's OK you have to understand them very emotional" he says.

A few minutes before all this Claire came out of the tent and whispered something to my Mom my Mom was sitting there singing this song she sings that I hate about a guy who plays the saxophone and he finally finds this great girlfriend but she goes somewhere and then they can't find each other again so I'm like shut up. Then Claire comes out and whispers I just hear the word "blood" and "panties". But I'm not an idiot unless the tent exploded and Claire got some kind of weird piece of tent stuck in her upper upper leg she's having her 1st Period. Which is fine with me I took Sex Ed in 8th grade and I know what's going on even though it was hard to think in Sex Ed you'd be trying to think but everyone was trying to be so mature all the time and not laugh and you'd have to look around to see who was going to laugh and pretty soon you didn't even remember the question then a girl would say "VAGINA" and everybody would be like "Hmm do I laugh now?" and before you know it all Hell breaks loose and it is not a learning environment. But it's pretty easy to deduce that Claires panties have her Period all over them.

Here's what my Mom looks like: She's medium height with brown hair that's short sometimes and long sometimes. She isn't big or small. She doesn't wear glasses. I don't know if she's pretty or not.

Anyway my Mom and my older sister Beth stood up and the 3 of them went into the tent Mom comes out later and says "everythings fine" and so Dad goes off to the bathroom which is about a 1/2 mile away by the ranger station not to go to the bathroom but because it's the only place with lights so he can read. My Dad loves to read I mean loves. You can hear him laughing from all that way over there because he's really into some book by a guy from England that he thinks is the funniest thing in the world and he laughs like crazy whenever he's reading it. He always tells us everything about what he's reading and when he was telling us about it he said it started with a scene of a guy "krepitating" which I had no idea what that was and I guess nobody else did either because we all looked at him which was when he informed us it actually means fart but he didn't say the word fart I think he said passing gas. Which is not usually what my Dad thinks is funny but I guess this guy was so smart he made it funny. My Dad by the way always wants me to read more and I think it's 1 of the great disappointments of his life that his only son me doesn't like to read every second but would rather do stuff including watch TV sometimes.

Anyway this incident is very symbolic of Claire becoming a woman and my summer and my whole family sometimes they just treat me like I'm some kind of moron. Even though I think they usually think I'm pretty smart. And the girls and Mom are always like "Oh you men" so I guess we do sort of gang up on them or something but I don't know what we're ganging up on them about.

Anyway later when I was already in bed Dad came in the tent. He got in his wooly underwear and lay down on top of his sleeping bag and put his hands behind his head and started breathing in very slowly through his nose and out through his mouth which is what he learned from a book called <u>Light On Yoga</u> by B.K.S. Iyengar for when you want to relax. I pretend to be asleep.

School was starting in a few days. Once when I was a kid and my Mom was sick my Dad made my lunch and he made sardines or more like he wrapped them up and I took them to school and ate them. Then I thought about Caroline Zisko. You know those girls who wear all black 100% of the time? That's Caroline black fish-net stockings through which you can see her legs but also you can't at the same time black pants black skirts black shirts. But her face is totally white so it's like all this black and then this white face coming out of it like a dead body. Kind of a good looking dead body though. She's got this blond hair that's really nice even though it looks like she never combs it or washes it her face is sort of pretty even though it's got these little pock marks all over it. Caroline was nice and I talked to her 1 time in 9th Grade it was near the end of the year and I was standing at the top of the stairs by the freshman lockers about to go home I guess it was Friday Caroline was walking by and then she stops and looks at me.

"So what are you doing this weekend?" she asked.

"Um I'm gonna go see a movie" I said pretty much because I knew "nothing" was a bad answer "nothing" was like "I never do anything I never have done anything not once with anybody."

"A movie. Cool" she said nodding her head up and down like she totally believed me.

And then she went down the stairs and right before she turned I saw her black T-shirt pulled very tight over her Breasts which were small but looked huge in that shirt.

I stood there and wondered if I should of said a specific movie like Raiders Of The Lost Ark. I wondered if there was any chance that she was going to invite me somewhere if I gave a different answer when she said "what are you doing this weekend?" or if maybe it wasn't a question but it was more like she wanted for me to ask her to do something like "I'm just hanging out want to go see Star Wars?" Or maybe she meant that her and a bunch of her friends (who all wore tons of eye-shadow everywhere and had gross yellow cigarette stains on their teeth that were supposed to be white) were going to hang out in a basement and light candles and play creepy music and they wanted me to come over and sit on the couch and hang out and even though they were weird and freaky they were kind of hot too.

My Dad was snoring now with lots of little whistles in it you could see the moon through the tent I didn't want to go to sleep because the summer even if it hadn't been so great was over. I thought about Coach Kurlyeskus huge forehead and everyone totally thirsty because in Romania you can't have any water until soccer practice is over and all of us about to puke from windsprints. I wondered if things would be different this year in 10th Grade I would make friends and kiss a girl and I would take a girls shirt off and all that stuff. I probably would in 10th Grade you're more settled in the High School environment and everything.

The next morning my Dad stuck his head in the tent and he was mad I was still sleeping and he said "Gnug" which is like Hungarian for "enough" (my Dad's not Hungarian I don't know why he says this 1 word in Hungarian). Because I was late all I got was granola bars sloshed down with powdery powdered milk then for 4 days we drove exactly exactly the speed limit not 1 mile over with my Dad concentrating on the highway and my Mom Not Smoking In The Car because my Dad won't let her smoke in the car so she put her arms in front of her then she put 1 leg over the other and put her nose and face between her finger and her thumb and then she put her legs up on the seat with her arms around them and her head on her knee trying to forget smoking. In the back Claire and Beth and me sat there I could feel all the Coke I had sloshing around in my stomach and we were too tired to do anything finally we pulled into the driveway and pretty much fell out of the car.

The next morning we went to the mall. When once in a million years my Dad goes to the mall with us we have meeting times and meeting places all of which is his specialty and also breaks for Orange Julius which he also believes in. I bought underpants and bags of socks because they are a better deal than buying separate socks pens small medium and large spiral notebooks 2-pocket folders for every subject plain paper lined paper graph paper and pencil sharpeners even though I never really use pencils. (I know there are supposed to be about 40 million commas in that sentence and everywhere else too but whenever I put them in they're in the wrong place so screw it. Mr. Rasfenjohn says the most important thing is to express yourself anyway. He's my Creative Comp I teacher. Most teachers every time you make a single mistake correct your whole paper so much you can't even see your paper anymore under all the corrections but Mr. Rasfenjohn might circle 1 place and put "do you want to use a comma here" because he doesn't want to interfere with your craft. Besides I'm not writing this for class anyway I'm just writing it. I'll just give myself an A on it.)

CHAPTER 2

1ST DAY OF SCHOOL

Here's what happened the 1st day of school. Even if you don't talk to too many people 1 on 1 you hear things when you're going up and down the halls and the 1st day of school I keep hearing people whispering stuff like "Japan" and "Tits" and "Blond" and "Blow." Normally that would all be pretty normal except for the Japan part but there was something weird going on everybody was really excited about something. Here's why:

Renee Shopmaker. Renee Shopmaker.

Renee Shopmaker. Renee Shopmaker. Renee Shopmaker. Renee Shopmaker. Renee Shopmaker. Renee Shopmaker.

Yes it was Renee Shopmaker. You'd know what I mean if you came out of 2nd Period Math II 1 day on the 1st day of school and you were walking down the hall and suddenly walking down the hall right past you was this incredible unbelievable girl with really long hair going way down her back in the back and very big Breasts and she was wearing believe it or not (you're pretty sure) a kimono. A purple 1.

But that didn't happen yet. 1st let me tell you something about Hutch Falls High everybody's got an attitude people are just very in to who they are and what they're like. The girls for instance are all running around the halls pulling their shirts down to show off their tans and they're giggling and they're just very pleased with who they are. Other girls like Beth of course are more moving around seeing every second who they can say "Welcome Back!!!!!" to and keeping track of how cool each person they talk to is. The jocks who in a sense I almost am 1 because I play soccer but I'm not really are standing around and they're like "Yo" and they think they're pretty cool and they just have all this attitude the real jocks usually play 2 sports like soccer and baseball or football and baseball or even tennis and I just play soccer but it's really more a state of mind the Jock State Of Mind which I don't have.

As for me I try to be more low key I don't think it's important to walk around acting like you're some big deal people should just go around being themselves and not make such a big deal out of it.

Also I think there's nothing wrong with not having a million friends I just think people are different and you don't always find people who are just like you right away. Especially around 7th and 8th Grade when everyone's dividing up into their groups and clicks with their friends and everything and already when we got to Hutch Falls Freshman Year the same groups from peoples other schools were pretty much set. So if things don't work out at 1 point they can still work out later.

Anyway the 1st thing the 1st day of school is orientation and welcome we're divided up into 2 auditoriums because there's too many people to fit into 1. The speakers speak in 1 auditorium then go to the other 1 and whoever was in the other 1 comes into that 1. 1 speaker is Mrs. Fammer the school psychologist who explains how to tell if your friends are about to commit suicide (1 way is if they start talking a lot about suicide). Then we get introduced to our Homeroom Instructors mine by the way is Mr. Dunne a physics teacher who teaches Physics I II III and IV. He isn't wearing it at the assembly but he always wears a white lab coat which I don't really get why because it's not like chemistry nothing's going to get on you or anything in Physics. After orientation I have World History. Then I have Math II. Tragically I have Mrs. Lippner for Math II who I had last year in Math I. She's younger than a lot of teachers and acts cool and everything but then gives quizzes every single week and gave me a D+ last year which was my only D ever and if I just got lucky and got in the other section I'd have Mr. Planjet who likes to be called Mr. Math and who has a big Afro even though he's white and has fun in class without tests.

After Math II I walked out into the hall. I was standing there deciding if I should go to my locker or not when she walked right past me. I was just there and then there she was going by. You may or may not believe that 1 moment can change your life. Philosophers have disagreed on this point. But I think it can and this is why I think I saw Renee and everything I believed before suddenly kind of disappeared. I know I didn't know her at all and had never said a word to her and as far as fate maybe never was going to but still it's true. And it wasn't just how beautiful she was I swear you could see something in the way she walked and moved and was and looked and everything that was her unique self and different from anybody else. I almost felt a cosmic thing even though I don't believe in that.

Of course by lunch she found John McKnight and Randy Brewer and Lenea Vovich and Cindy Tollson and all the people you know she's going to be friends with. I'm wondering what if I went up to her before she met anyone and said "Hey! Welcome to Hutch Falls!" Maybe then fate would be different maybe you can change fate. But basically John and Randy and her would be like "Sorry but she's OBVIOUSLY going to be our friend" and I would be like "I know".

So the day was weird because it's the 1st day of school anyway and then I'm thinking about her all day the word is already out that her father is some kind of businessman and they lived in Japan where he was doing business until they just came back.

Anyway Spanish is my last period class. We have Spanish in the language center which is basically a regular classroom except there's posters all over the place of bullfighters and French wine and ruins. There's this 1 poster with a bullfighter in this dress almost and he's staring at this bull that's running at him and under the picture the poster says "JUAN RAMI-REZ LEGENDARY SPANISH BULLFIGHTER". Freshman Year I spent a lot of time in Spanish looking at that.

So I go in and see Juan Ramirez and I'm looking at him for a second and then I see something purple. The new girl is just about the only purple thing around but there's no way she's in my Spanish class and I look up and there she is sitting down in a chair in the back of the room. I always sit in the back so no one can think anything's weird about me sitting down behind her and 1 row over so I just sit down and I've got this perfect view where I can see her Breasts from the side and the way they're making this huge almost like a hill in her kimono not to be a pervert.

The bell rings and Mr. Eller comes in he was our Spanish teacher Freshman Year too. He's pretty young for a teacher but he used to teach at a college in New York and he's pretty uptight he wears suits every day and Freshman Year he used to kick this 1 girl Lucy Blum out of class every single day for talking without raising her hand I'm not exaggerating or trying to be funny.

So Mr. Eller comes in and right away he says "Buenos Dias."

"Buenos Dias" we all say at the same time.

Mr. Eller nods with contentment then he goes right up to Serena Isaacson who everyone knows is the smartest student in the class. He says "Como Estas?"

Serena waits a second then she says "Bien Gracias."

Everybody's relieved because now we're sure what to say

after a whole summer of no Spanish so now Mr. Eller goes up to everybody and asks "Como Estas" and everybody says "Bien Gracias" or "<u>Muy</u> Bien Gracias" depending on how good they are. Except for this 1 guy Robbie who Mr. Eller calls "Pepito" who says "Yo Estoy Muy Bien" but he's so happy about saying the "Yo Estoy" part he forgets to say "Gracias" and Mr. Eller has to say "Gracias?" Then he says "Gracias."

Then Mr. Eller gets to the new girl. He says "Como Estas?" And she says "Bien Gracias". I'm trying to figure out how she learned Spanish in Japan and if maybe she's some kind of language genius and then Mr. Eller says "how do you say "how are you" in Japanese?" so even the teachers basically know this hot new girl is here from Japan and from the side I can see she's opening her mouth but not a lot and her lips get screwed up kind of and she sticks her head out and goes "hap-shphshfeee" or something like that and it's different sounding and really really beautiful. I want her to say it again just so I can hear her say it again.

Next we get divided up for dialogue drill usually you end up with whoever's in front of you as your partner for dialogue drill but the seat behind Renee Shopmaker is empty and everything gets fucked up and Mr. Eller points to me and to her.

"You 2" he says.

Suddenly everybody's standing up there's no time to think and I just take my chair and take it over to her desk and sit down.

"Hi" she says.

"Hey."

"I'm Renee."

"Hi I'm Jeremy."

She's got perfume on and I can't stop smelling it.

"Begin dialogue" Mr. Eller says.

Neither of us says anything. Then I realize that as the man and as the senior Spanish student I have to do something.

"Um Buenos Dias" I say.

I know it's bad but I say "um" a lot sometimes when I don't know what to say because for example I'm speaking Spanish and I don't speak Spanish.

"Buenos Dias" she says.

There's a very very long silence.

"Como" she says finally and then she thinks for a second and then she says "Estas?"

"Bien." I forget for a second and then I say "Gracias."

Then I wonder if I should impress her with a "Muy" but it's too late.

There's another very long pause and then I say "Como Como Estas" accidentally repeating the Como like a total idiot.

"Bien" she says right away. Then she says "Oh. Gracias."

Then we sit there. Most of the other people in the class are finished too and we wait for Mr. Eller to announce the dialogue drill is over.

Anyway at soccer practice everyone is talking about her and I don't say anything we all suck from having the whole summer off except for Chris Halal who went to soccer camp. We're not in shape either and Coach Kurlyesku is pissed but finally practice ends.

After practice I rode home with Anthony Rey a senior on the Varsity who's a pretty cool guy and who lives a couple blocks down from us when Anthony drops me off he says "Later" and I say "Later" and I picture him and Eric Loff and Ben Luzano and Terry Hogan sitting around in 1 of their basements on Friday night drinking beers and saying "Later" to each other over and over and over again. I don't know how anybody ever actually leaves. Because they're so busy saying it.

I go in the back like I do every day and my Mom's in the kitchen cooking some smelly fish because that's all we ever eat. She's wearing a brown shirt with no sleeves that she wears a lot she looks kind of bored and when I come in she says "How was school?"

"Fine" I say.

"Do you like not being a Freshman anymore?"

This is a typical my Mom question everything's kind of upside-down. So I have to think for a second to figure it out.

"I guess" I say.

"Did you make any new friends?" she asks.

"I don't have time for new friends" I say.

"You should bring your friends over this year" she says.

I say "I've told you a million times people don't hang out at peoples houses."

She says "I know I know but you're getting older and if you ever want to bring anyone over for dinner I just want you to know that's fine people like to come over for dinner."

"Not when all you eat is fish" I say.

"Well your father" she says and that's all she says.

I go up to my room I don't even take my shoes off I just lie down on my bed. I only have 1 poster up in my room and it's my Charlies Angels poster and it's right over my bed so I look up at it. (Back in 8th Grade when I asked my Mom if I could put it up here's what she said:

"Who are Charlies Angels?" she said.

"They're like detectives" I said.

"Detectives?" she said.

"On TV."

"Who's Charlie?"

"He's sort of their boss."

"Why are they called Angels?"

"I don't know."

"Well it's your room do whatever you want."

She said that but I could tell she didn't like it but I didn't really know what it was exactly she didn't like. Either my putting tape on the walls or posters in general or detectives or hot women who dressed in hot clothes and jumped around and showed their Breasts off a lot? Anyway I put it up on the wall but I was afraid about what she was thinking about what I was thinking about them which I wasn't.)

So I look up at the Angels now and I think about what they were like in High School probably like Lenea and Cindy and then they just grew up into detectives and women with Breasts like that and everything. Then I put my hands behind my head and just stared contemplating at the ceiling. I was thinking about if I was running up and down hills in Japan and it was getting dark and there were all these Samurais all over the place and they've got these huge horses and I'm chopping their heads off and they're falling on the ground and rolling around. I've got this huge sword the kind with a curve in it and I'm getting blood all over my blue Alligator shirt which I realize is stupid so I imagine I'm in chainmail and armor except not on my face because I want to be able to see and then there's this castle and it's on fire and I'm climbing up these huge walls to get in and there are all these screaming ladies inside with the very white faces and they're wearing kimonos and some of them have sushi which is Japanese raw fish and Renee's right in the middle of them all and I grab her and get her out of there and then we go outside in the woods and Renee puts her head on my shoulder and she smells nice and she says "I'm so tired." I make up stuff like that sometimes.

I remember Miss Lander my 3rd Grade teacher she was very skinny and she wore these skirts in 3rd Grade sometimes I used to think about her a lot and miss her on the weekend. Then I pictured myself kissing Renee Shopmaker and by the way she's so hot nobody even notices her name which is like what is a Shopmaker? In Medieval and ancient times people from other countries have names which are indications of what they do for a living like John Carpenter who's a carpenter or Bob Cabinetmaker but what's a Shopmaker she makes Shops? How do you make a shop? This name could be her 1 weakness like Superman had Kryptonite and Achilles from The Odyssey has a fucked up heel but she's so hot NOBODY EVEN NOTICES like if Lex Luthor was holding a huge hunk of Kryptonite over Superman and he was dying and then Lex suddenly said "Oh Superman you're so great" and dropped the Kryptonite and forgot about it. Anyway I stopped thinking about kissing her. That would never happen Mrs. Lippner could probably come up with an algebra equation that proves that would never ever happen and I could smell the fish my

Mom was making downstairs but even if I liked fish which I don't I wasn't that hungry anyway.

There was a long road ahead of me. With obstacles like Geometry. And soccer games. These are the challenges I needed to face on the night of the 1st day of school.

CHAPTER 3

I MEET GILLIAN

I'm sitting outside in the courtyard at 1 of the tables out there in the morning it rained pretty hard so it's wet and nobody else is outside and the tables are covered with these berries that fall off the trees and mush all over everything out there. I'm wearing my soccer jacket and I figure I look like 1 of those outdoor types who just like it outside all the time. This is several weeks after the beginning of school by the way.

I've got this meat loaf my Mom's wrapped up in enough tin foil to protect it from an atom bomb and I'm about 1/2 way through unwrapping it when I hear someone say "Can we sit here?" I look up and there's this girl standing there behind her is Caroline Zisko. Who by the way I haven't talked to at all this year she's got on a black sweater made out of Angora that looks like it's sort of coming apart and sticking out of itself and for some reason when you look at it all you want to do is touch it and the girl in it whoever she is (Angora is very soft). She's really thin this year and her blond hair is about 1/2 black now she looks old her face is still really white though and she's wearing this purple black lipstick that makes her look like some kind of mummy. And behind her there's a guy in glasses standing. I've seen him but I don't know him.

"Yeah" I say.

Sometimes when it's really crowded people sit with people they don't really know and then I look at my sandwich like it's fascinating or something and try not to listen to them but there are tables everywhere now because it's wet.

They all sit down when I say it's OK. The 1st girl I don't know is close to me Caroline's next to her and the guy is around the other side. The 1st girl looks kind of flat and she's got a lot of brown hair more than usual and it's very curly I'm pretty sure she's new this year and I've seen her around in the halls a few times during the past few weeks. In fact once or twice I think she looked at me in a funny way sort of like she knew me from somewhere or something. Anyway she opens up a carton of chocolate milk then she says "I'm Gillian."

"I'm Jeremy" I say.

"So you know Caroline right?" she says.

"Yeah."

"Hi Jeremy" Caroline says.

"Hey."

"How was your summer?"

"Good how was your summer?" I said.

"Ugh don't even ask" Caroline says shaking her head.

"That's Douglas" Gillian says.

"Hey" I say.

He nods he's got this kind of round face and there's a little bit of hairy beard on it that makes him look a little like he writes poetry or needs a shave. He also looks pissed off not at me but at the world or something.

"What is that?" Gillian says pointing at my lunch which looks very gross and making a face.

"Meat loaf."

"Oh" she said. Then she said "Isn't that more like dinner food?"

"It was" I say. "Last night."

Gillian laughs and Caroline laughs and I realize I made a pretty good joke.

I was thinking about how it's weird because with this group because they're rebellious or whatever and different in their black clothes and non-participating in extra-curricular activities people might think I was sitting with them. There was a long pause and all 3 of them were staring at me especially the guy Douglas.

"I don't eat meat" Caroline says she takes a cucumber out of a baggie and holds it up.

"Do you always bring lunch?" Gillian says.

"Yeah my Mom makes it" I say and then I feel stupid because don't most people make their own lunch?

"My Mom can't even make a sandwich" Gillian says.

"What do you eat?" I ask.

"We go to a restaurant called Olives a lot."

Eating out a lot is not a good sign of family togetherness.

Caroline says "My Mom cooks but it's all like hello do you know I'm a vegetarian?" She put a piece of celery between her 2 lips.

"What do you eat? Just vegetables?" I asked her.

"Pretty much. And fruit, and yogurt, and cereal. I like cereal for dinner Grape Nuts they're good."

"My Dad eats Shredded Wheat" I say.

"What is he like constipated?" Caroline asks.

"What?" I say.

"Isn't that what people who have to go to the bathroom eat?"

"I don't think so."

Just then some wind came out of nowhere and knocked some rain out of the trees. Gillian had to shake her head a few times to get the water out of all her hair which she has a lot of. Douglas wiped off his sandwich. Gillian looked at me and said really seriously "So why are you eating out here?"

"I like the outdoors" I said.

"But it's raining."

"It wasn't before."

"It was going to."

"I just really like the outdoors."

Gillian looked at me like that was kind of lame but before I could say anything Caroline said "Did you do the history?" to Douglas. And I looked over at them like I thought me and Gillian were supposed to be listening to them.

"Yes I did the history" Douglas said. Sarcastically. This was the 1st time I'd heard him say anything and he was 1 of those guys who doesn't look like it but has a really really deep voice.

"What's it about?" Caroline asked.

"The Industrial Revolution."

"What about it?"

"Everything about it."

"Well what is it exactly? Is it like industry?"

Douglas put down his sandwich now and stared at her face. "Bergoff talked about it for 45 minutes on Monday" he said.

"Yeah well. I wasn't paying attention" Caroline said.

"What the fuck were you doing?"

"You'll have to excuse Douglas he's in 1 of his moods" Gillian said to me.

"I don't know" said Caroline.

Douglas looks at her.

"So what is it?" Caroline said.

Douglas says "Let's put it this way. Your whole life would be different if there were no Industrial Revolution. Your clothes would be made by hand there'd be no cars so we wouldn't even live in fucking Hutch Falls because there'd be no such thing. Without cars."

"Where would we live?" Caroline asked.

Douglas said "I don't know on farms. With cows. It would suck."

"This doesn't suck?" said Caroline.

Douglas picked up his sandwich and looked at it like he was thinking. Caroline turned to me.

"You're on the soccer team this year right?" she said.

"Yeah last year too."

"Are you guys any good?"

"We're 4 and 2."

Nobody said anything and then Caroline says to Gillian "Where's Kath?"

"I don't think she's here. Was she in math?"

"She's sick" says Douglas.

"She's sick every other day" Gillian says to me.

"That depends on what you mean by sick" Douglas says.

"Not here" Gillian says.

Douglas sort of grunts. I don't even know who Kath is and while they're talking about her I wonder why Carolines summer was so bad you can't ask about it then all of a sudden they're like "OK" and Caroline and Douglas crumble up their garbage and put it on Gillians tray.

"What do you have after lunch?" Gillian says looking at me.

"Math Sociology and Spanish."

"Ola" says Caroline and she starts laughing.

I didn't know if she wanted me to answer her? In Spanish? I was about to say "Buenos Dias" when Gillian said "OK let's go."

"I need a cig" said Caroline.

All 3 of them stand up and Gillian looks at me and says "So when's your next game?"

"Monday Holy Brothers Of Saint Christopher" I say.

Gillian says "OK see you later."

"Yeah. Later" I say.

And then they walked back into the Lunchroom.

CHAPTER 4

THE BIG GAME

Holy Brothers Of Saint Christopher is our really big rival.
They're a religious school and Hutch Falls is about 3
times as big so you'd think we'd cream them every time but
either they've got God on their side or something because the
games are always tight. Also you'd think religious people would
be really nice or sportsmanlike or wimpy or something but
that is not what religious people are like even a little they go
after the ball like God told them to and they don't mind flying
face 1st into the ground and they keep playing even if their
heads bleeding or their knees coming out the other side of
their leg.

Right before the game Coach Kurlyesku tells me to come
to his office. This is bad because it usually means 1 of your
teachers went to Coach Kurlyesku and asked him to light a
fire under your ass by telling you you are in danger of not
being allowed to play soccer anymore unless you pick up the

slack in their lame anyway class. This never happened to me before because last year when I was getting my D+ in math it was 2nd Semester and there was no soccer. But now it's happening because I got a D and a D− on 2 quizzes in guess what Math. In most classes I get Bs and sometimes Cs. (Last year on 1 of my written evaluations in a class where I got a C my teacher wrote my thinking deserved a B but my work deserved a C.) This is probably above average. But my Dad thinks a B is mediocre versus what the school officially says which is it's good and he thinks a C is like an F− or a G. The worst grade he ever got was a B on a test in law school when he had bubonic plague or something and passed out 1/2 way through the test and still got a B. My Mom thinks I haven't found myself academically. Anyway I got the D and the D− on the quizzes in math partly because I suck at math and partly because I don't do the homework always because you shouldn't be forced to do things you're naturally not intended by God to do in terms of how he made your brain and personality. We're all special.

So I go to Coach Kurlyeskus office which is in the hall right by the locker room he's got lots of trophies and baseball bats and crap all over the place and no windows and it feels weird inside because it's not an office office when the person in there is a coach and doesn't really do any work like real teachers and people in offices but it also makes it kind of cool to be there too and talk about sports and stuff like you would never do in a real teachers office but also you know the difference between when you're in there because you helped Coach carry some balls or something back from the bus and you can hang out and talk for a minute and when you're in there because you're in trouble. When I go in Coach Kurlyesku's there behind his desk in 1 of his trademark sweatsuits which is a lot more like a Romanian type sweatsuit than Adidas or anything. "Sit down" he says but it sounds like "Seet down." I'm supposed to describe stuff so let me describe Coach Kurlyesku. Basically he's got a really big forehead. He looks like 1 of those guys from ancient times like Australeopithacus man. He's also from Romania and you can only understand 1/2 of what he says but he gets mad if you say "what" so you have to pretend to understand everything.

So I seet down.

He says "Jermee work more in math."

"OK" I say.

"Now Jermee before beeg game I have question. Why why" and his forehead is crunching up all of a sudden like he's the most confused person on the planet "Why yooo keeek ball fast? I want yooo I want yooo slow. Theeenk. Weeth ball. So yooo get ball good like real player. But zen" and Coach Kurlyesku puts his hands up and sort of waves his fingers around and goes "Aaaah!" really loud. I've never seen him do this before and I'm pretty surprised and I just stare at him. Then he points at me and says "Why yooo fast? Slow slow. Theeenk theeenk. Pass! Zen meekaboo."

Except for Meekaboo I think I get the idea of what he's saying and I say "But you're always yelling at the fullbacks to get rid of the ball."

He says "No fullback. Zem. No. Yooo yooo keeep ball keeep ball OK?"

"OK" I say.

And then I leave.

I go to the locker room and everybodys there already everybodys acting all cool like it's just another game but you can sort of tell even John McKnight and Randy Brewer and those guys are a little nervous after all the odds of getting a broken face or something and then losing too when you play Holy Brothers Of Saint Christopher are pretty good.

We go through the tunnel to the field. The tunnel smells like old underwear with lemons. I don't know why. When we hit the field the whole crowd is already there and it's the hugest crowd we've had yet this year by a long shot and there are people on both sides of the field and even all over the end-lines so we warm up with passing drills and shots on goal and all this stuff you always do without even thinking about it be-lieve me you think a lot more with all these people there. The sun is on its way down and it's getting kind of cold out but it feels good and you get that feeling like you can run forever and kick the ball really far that you get when it's not hot.

The Refs blow their whistles and we start. Holy Brothers is attacking really hard right away and we've got everybody back I break up a few dribbles and knock some guys off the ball but I keep booting it up the field totally forgetting what Coach Kurlyesku said to me and then I remember pretty much a 10th of a second later after I kick it and I'm like "Ugh." Over on the sidelines I see Renee with Lenea and Cindy standing there and a lot of other girls all around them and most of them are wearing skirts. Last year they all went to football games not soccer. Cindy was a cheerleader but she broke her ankle and she still can't cheerlead this year while it's recuperating and her and all the girls got to know John McKnight better and fell in love with him so now they're all soccer fans and at every game and they scream whenever John or Randy Brewer touches the ball it doesn't even matter if they screw up they cheer for them just because they're them I guess. As for me I could steal the ball from a forward on a break-away then dribble down field through every Holy Brother there was and do a reverse bicycle kick into the goal and nobody would say anything.

Anyway nobody scores and the games going on and sometimes when I look over I see Renees Breast which is so big sideways and also Leneas hair which is long and black and gets stuck in the wind and goes blowing out sideways at a 90 Degree angle and Cindy Tollson. Renee a lot of times is saying something to 1 of them. Or laughing really hard where she puts her hands on her knees and looks like she's going to fall over or maybe throw up. 2 different times I was looking too long at them and I suddenly got this feeling like uh-oh something's happening and the ball was about 2 feet away from me and I booted it up the field and I heard Coach Kurlyesku from the sidelines go "Slooow! Slooow!"

It's tied 0-0 at half-time we're standing around the cooler and I'm drinking Gatorade and looking around and I see Gillian and Caroline and that guy Douglas all the way down behind the goal by the parking lot they're hard to see because they'd rather die than wear any bright colors or anything. I think Gillian waves at me but I'm not sure so I just kind of look without waving back like I might be looking at something else behind them and didn't see her wave. It looks like they're all smoking right there in front of all the teachers and parents and everybody. I don't get how they're not going to get in trouble. In case they're watching I turn back around

like I have to talk to my teammates about the game and everything like there's some big strategy we have to plan for the
2nd 1/2 if we're going to win.

Anyway God or not I think Holy Brothers is tired from
going so crazy in the 1st 1/2 and we're in front of their goal
more in the 2nd 1/2 but it's still 0-0 until about 15 minutes left
in the game when Chris Halal sprints in from mid-field takes
a pass from Randy on the wing and scores a goal we all go
pretty much nuts and the crowd is going crazy and I go give
Chris a Hi-5 and so does everybody else.

Holy Brothers suddenly gets possessed by the Devil now
because they're going to lose and they're back going crazy all
over our backfield like their lives depended on it and they
aren't tired now all of a sudden. I slide under a Holy Brothers
forward and knock the ball he's got out of bounds I hear
Coach Kurlyesku shouting "Goood goood goood." I check the
same man on the throw in and the ball goes back to mid-field
and I get in front of him the ball comes up to a halfback in
front of me and he wants to blast it past me down the wing to
my man. I see him kick the ball and it's coming right at me
and I want to stop it but it's going way too fast to get my foot
up and too low to get my chest on it and then I want to get out
of the way and I hear "whoooosh" and the ball flies into my
balls and I fall completely down on the ground. I can't really
breathe much and I'm bent in 2 pieces and I hear people talking and I wonder if anyone scored and I roll onto my back and
John McKnight is next to me bending down. His hair's all
sweaty which I wouldn't normally notice but I notice now because everything looks huge and right in my face and it's
stuck to his forehead. He goes "Man. Ouch." Then he picks

up my hand and puts it on my stomach and says "hold up the waistband of your shorts it helps." I hold it up and it helps but like when your head's on fire and somebody puts out 1 little piece of it but not the rest so you're still on fire and Coach Kurlyesku is looking down at me and I wonder if Renee is watching and I picture her maybe going "Wow". John McKnight is standing up now and he's still looking at me and for a few seconds lying there surrounded by everyone and all the Holy Brothers Of Saint Christopher with some tears I can't do anything about going down my face and my balls pretty much crushed everything felt kind of OK. It was weird.

Anyway Coach Kurlyesku came out and everybody was discussing if I needed a stretcher and an ambulance but finally I was like "I can make it" and Chris Halal and Coach Kurlyesku each took 1 of my arms and helped me get up. Getting up hurt about as much as getting the ball in the balls in the 1st place or maybe more because it took longer. I walked very slowly to the sidelines with them almost carrying me and then I sat down and then I lied down and the game started again. I could turn my head and see legs running around. Nobody else scored and pretty soon it was over.

After the game I got a lot of sympathy in the locker room. We won so everybody was happy and in a really good mood but every time Randy walked by me he shook his head and said "ultimate sacrifice ultimate sacrifice" and some other guys picked it up too and started saying it.

I had my soccer jacket on and my white Adidas bag over my shoulder and when I limped out into the parking lot I felt sort of tough for having won and survived and given the ultimate sacrifice and all. The parking lot was very crowded with all the fans and everything. Over at the teachers spaces Coach Kurlyesku was standing next to his car which is a green Pinto and has soccer balls and nets and bags and stuff in the back all the time and he's smiling this huge smile which you don't see much and talking to parents probably about the game. John and Randy were over talking to Renee and Lenea and Cindy and they were all all over them and I was sure saying how great they were (even though Chris scored the winning goal) Lenea and Cindy especially because Renee isn't as loud as they are she just doesn't make a big deal out of everything. John is standing right next to Renee and they're talking. Basically they're pre-destined to be like the Romeo and Juliet of Hutch Falls High. Except for not dying at the end. (Which is a very overrated book in my opinion. I wanted to write my English paper with the thesis "Romeo and Juliet totally sucks." You're supposed to give supporting examples. 1 supporting example of it sucking would be you can't understand anything Shakespeare says. Here is an example from Act 3 Scene 4 of not understanding it:

It best agrees with night. Come, civil night,
Thou sober-suited matron all in black,
And learn me how to lose a winning match
Played for a pair of stainless maidenhoods.
Hood my unmanned blood, bating in my cheeks,
With thy black mantle till strange love grow bold,
Think true love acted simple modesty.

WHAT?? ?? Do you under-

stand anything this guy is saying? No you don't. Another example of it sucking is the plot Romeo thinks Juliet is dead because she drinks this magic potion that makes you seem like
you're dead when you're not so he drinks poison and kills
himself. This is totally unrealistic because 1st of all there's no
magic potion that does that 2nd of all if there was don't you
think people would know about it by now? so wouldn't Romeo
instead of suddenly killing himself be like "Hmm Maybe she
took that magic potion I better wait a few hours before poi-
soning myself to death." Give me a break. 3rd of all what
about Juliet knowing Romeo's dead when she wakes up? How
does she? I mean she just took the magic potion why doesn't
she think maybe Romeo took the magic potion I should make
sure he's really dead before stabbing myself to death. What a
couple of idiots. By the way my thesis ended up being
"Romeo and Juliet is 1 of Shakespeares greatest plays" which
I got a C− on anyway because Mr. Trudett said I should of
mentioned some of Shakespeares other plays.)

Anyway I didn't have a ride home so I was going to walk or
limp I guess and I started going across the parking lot and
everyone all over was in such a good mood about winning.
Then I see Gillian and Caroline and that same guy Douglas.
Gillian's wearing this dark red sweater and she's got red lipstick on and she's still pretty flat. She's looking right at me as
I go by them and I'm still pretty far away and she goes "Hi"
and I stop. A part of me thinks maybe they're waiting for me
or something because I did tell them about the game but they
don't really act like they're waiting for me or anything and
Caroline is smoking away on a "cig" again totally not worried
about anybody seeing her and Douglas has shaved and he

looks kind of like he has a different sort of more normal personality now. I say "Hey." Gillian goes "Are you OK?" And we're kind of shouting because we're sort of far away but I don't want to go over like I think they're waiting there for me or something. So I say pretty loud "Yeah."

"That had to hurt" Douglas screamed.

"Yeah" I said.

"Do you want a cigarette?" Caroline says and I can see Gillian look at her like "what are you asking him that for?"

"No thanks" I said.

And I'm starting to feel stupid talking so far away and I hear some people laughing behind me and cars are starting to drive around the parking lot and go out the front towards home or wherever they're going and I'm pretty close to where Renee and those guys are hanging out with each other and I wonder if they see me talking to these guys and then I hear "Jeremy would you like a ride home?" I look and Mrs. Shalquist is looking at me out the window of her car her sons a freshman and they live pretty close to us and I say "Yeah" and I look back over at Gillian and everybody and Gillian smiles and I give a little sort of stupid wave and then I get in the car and we go.

Let me tell you right now as we drive through Hutch Falls that it's a wonderful place to raise a family. It has many of the advantages of the city like restaurants and culture but also has low crime and other problems like dirt. Some kids are always like "This sucks!" about everything but they'd hate it anywhere and there is also a variety of people. I guess wherever you live you're like This Is My Universe but Hutch Falls is a place I'll always remember. In particular also places like Nierbeck Woods and the movie theater are cool and you don't have that anywhere else.

There's a yard behind our house and you can see some of the other yards on the block and in the summer people are out there a lot bar-b-qing and playing with their dogs and playing Frisbee. But now it was definitely Fall and cold so no one was out and I was sitting there on the tree swing my Dad put up when I was a kid and it was about the most macho Dad-type thing he ever did and I still remember how happy he was when he took me out there and showed it to me I think it was like he'd built our whole house by himself to him. You could still smell peoples dinner from other houses on our street especially potatoes and carrots and stuff like that if you looked at some of the windows they were blue from the TV going. The pain in my balls was getting better but it still hurt if I moved. I kept thinking about Coach Kurlyesku telling me to go slow I don't know why but something about Coach Kurlyesku makes me think he's 1 of the teachers who I like better than the other teachers which is weird because I swear to God the guy doesn't even talk much. The 1st day of soccer practice last year and that's his 1st year at Hutch Falls he showed us this movie of a World Cup soccer game from 1970. "You must see great Pele" he keeps saying like we didn't hear him the 1st 10,000 times he said it. Anyway Pele scores the winning goal with about 2 seconds left in the game he dribbles around all the fullbacks from the other team and then makes a perfect shot right into the corner of the net. So later we have this big debate in the locker room and we decide Coach Kurlyesku is the last fullback Pele went around he was younger and he had very long hair and he looked like a hippie but we were pretty sure it was him. We figured he was really embarrassed about Pele going around him so he didn't want us to know. So nobody said anything.

Sitting there swinging away on the tire swing I started to wonder if Pele said anything to Coach Kurlyesku after that game. Like "Coach Kurlyesku I am sorry for dribbling around you." I wondered if Renee saw any of the good plays I made. Things happened pretty fast so I understood if maybe she didn't. Maybe she'd say something about it the next day in Spanish like "You were so great." Maybe I'd just sit down with her and her friends at lunch I pictured what they'd do. They'd be about as surprised as if a huge elephant walked into the Lunchroom and sat down.

CHAPTER 5

THE MALL

My Dad calls The Mall a big vacuum cleaner for money. When you tell him you're going he just looks at you and you wait a second and then sure enough he says "it's just a big vacuum cleaner for money" like he never said it before or sometimes he just says "don't get vacuumed."

I'm not a major mall person anyway it's just all the same people from school going there and doing nothing and I'm not into that but I usually go on Saturday or Sunday or if there's nothing else to do both.

I went on Saturday after the Holy Brothers game. My Dad of course stayed home (to read) and as soon as we got there my Mom and Beth went to look at bedspreads or something for bedrooms and I started walking around alone with Claire. Claire is very cool she is 5 Foot 2 and has black hair and sad eyes. We went up to see what was going on at McDonalds (1 great mystery is why McDonalds isn't in the Food Court with all the rest of the restaurants). Then we went to The Limited Claire wanted to find a blue dress for this Halloween Dance at her Middle School she was going to I was psyched to go because there are always a million girls there they talk about The Limited all the time too at school like "It's from The Limited" and "Oh I got this at The Limited" or "They've got the cutest <u>fill in any type of girls clothes you want here</u> at The Limited." Inside Another 1 Bites The Dust is playing which goes:

Another 1 Bites The Dust
Another 1 Bites The Dust
Another 1 Bites The Dust Hey Hey
Another 1 Bites The Dust

and the whole place feels like Europe or something because of the fluorescent lights like at school but darker. Sales ladies in tight sweaters are everywhere and a lot of girls but from schools all over because I don't recognize most of them. Let me describe my clothes. I should of worn my soccer jacket but for whatever reason I just wore a green Alligator shirt there are mirrors everywhere so you see yourself every 10 seconds and my hair's very curly so it always looks messy. My Aunt Ruth said once it was like I had a birds nest on my head but I don't think about my hair much.

"Jeremy" Claire says.

She's holding this blue dress up to herself. Claire's very small partly because she's young partly because she's just small and she's got the curly black hair like me but it looks good on a girl and she's got a very dark face so sometimes total strangers ask her if she's from Greece. She could probably be the Lenea or Cindy of her class if she wanted to but she's too good for that that's versus Beth who would give her life to be the Lenea or Cindy of her class but could never even come close. But she's always trying and it's pathetic in the way she's always hanging around certain girls and hoping to be like them. Claire holds the blue dress up and I think it looks good but I don't say anything because I'm a guy and what do guys know about it. Except she says "do you like it?" so then I say "definitely" and then she puts it back anyway proving what I said.

Claire's looking around and I'm looking around and believe me there isn't much for a guy to look around at in The Limited except the hot girls from all over who don't know me at all. Then I look up and Claire's gone and there's this girl in my aisle looking at sweaters for a second I think she's about 23 because she's got this very straight red-brown hair that's feathered and this face and she just seems old but then I realize I'm crazy and she's my age too. She's checking out sweaters and I suddenly wonder what I'll say if she asks me what the hell I'm doing there and I suddenly wish again I was wearing my special occasion corduroys which are blue and I got Freshman Year and I keep in my bottom drawer and never wear to just The Mall and my soccer jacket.

I'm running out of girls sweaters to look at like I'm looking for my girlfriend or something and I keep looking at the girl and her hair and she's wearing Calvin Klein jeans just like Amanda Posher wore every single day in 8th Grade and her butt is really round in them just like Amandas was and her Breasts are really pointy in this very orange sweater she's wearing and

I see her start to look over at me and I look back at the sweaters fast then I sort of freeze and she starts to go behind me and she's tall not as much as me but more than most girls and the aisles are very thin because there are sweaters everywhere and I just feel some part of her kind of touch me a little on my back as she goes by. Her Breasts I think. Or maybe her arm or shoulder or something not on purpose and then she goes off to another part of the store.

"Do you like her?"

Claire's next to me all of a sudden.

"What?"

"Do you like her?"

"She's OK" I say.

"You should go talk to her."

"You have to play it cool" I say.

Claire gives me this look she gives me sometimes that's like "You're my brother but you're a total moron".

Claire doesn't find a dress she wants and we head out of The Limited. We go to the big center part of the 2nd floor at the end over the Food Court. There's a big long hole down the middle of the 2nd and 3rd floors here so you can look down to the 1st floor I'm always picturing someone falling over the side and then splatting down on the floor downstairs about an inch from the big fountain there that could of saved them if they'd landed in it. I wonder if that happened if I could jump over before they kept falling and keep 1 hand on the railing and grab them with the other hand so they'd be hanging there and pull them back up and over and then myself. You'd have to time it perfectly. Anyway there are benches and big plants all over we sit down and Claire doesn't say anything and then she says "I heard Mom and Dad talking last night."

"Yeah?" I said.

"About college."

"Fuck college." I don't say anything then I say "I'm not even going."

"You're not?"

"Nope."

"Does Dad know?"

"No."

"He'll flip."

We sat there for a second then Claire says "How come you're not going?"

"It's just what everyone does for no reason except everyone's doing it" I said.

Right around then I look around and I see Gillian and Carolines friend Douglas going by. He sees me and he stops. He's wearing his glasses.

"Hello" he says.

"Hey" I say.

He looks at Claire then he says to me "We're meeting at the Food Court in a couple minutes."

I nod and I say "cool." He goes down the escalator and Claire stands up and says "Go be with your friends."

"Do you think?" I say.

"He was definitely inviting you."

Claire goes off to look for Mom and Beth and I go into B. Dalton because he said they weren't meeting for a couple minutes I stood by the magazines. The ones for women always have models on them and they're fake smiling but you can see a lot of cleavage. They have tons of make-up on too which I don't like. My Dad loves bookstores and should love B. Dalton because it's got so many books except it's in the mall so even though if he has to go to the mall with us for something he'll spend all his time in B. Dalton he won't go to the mall just to go there he'd rather go to a bookstore somewhere else including especially a used 1 where everything's cheaper.

Then I go downstairs. I can't even stand 1/2 the stuff in the Food Court like the fruit drinks with 50 kinds of fruit in them and Steak 'N Brew and really bad wet cheese and sausage pizzas but anyway there are about a 100 tables in the middle of the Food Court and food all along both sides. I'm looking for them and it's totally packed and I don't see them but then I see them pretty far back by King Burger which I guess is where they would sit because it's the grosser part of the Food Court in the back with King Burger and Orange Julius and all the stuff that's been there since The Mall opened. Versus the salad place "Salad Patch" and the Frogurt place "Frogurt" up in front where you're more likely to see Lenea Vovich throwing her hair around and with a straw in her mouth drinking a fruit drink like she thinks she's on the deck of a big cruise ship or something like The Queen Elizabeth.

So they're sitting back there and I start to walk towards them but suddenly I'm not sure if Gillian and Caroline know Douglas invited me and if they're psyched or if they were like "Why'd you invite him???" and there's another kind of very plump girl sitting there with them too and I'm getting ready to cut out and go to King Burger like that's where I was going anyway when Gillian looks at me and says "Hi."

So I keep going and I walk up to them and stop.

"Hey" I say.

The other girl who's the girl Kath they were talking about at lunch the other day says "I'm Kath."

She crunches her face up like she feels bad about something like if she just hit you in the face with a baseball bat or something.

I say "Hey. I'm Jeremy."

"Douglas get a chair" Gillian orders him and Douglas pulls a chair over from another table and before I know it I'm sitting down between Gillian and Kath with Caroline and Douglas. Caroline of course is in all black and Gillian is wearing blue jeans and she looks different than at school even the way she's sitting is like she's a little more something but she has the same red lipstick on her big lips.

"How are your balls?"

Kath said that and then she giggled and put her hands up in front of her face but not that same sorry face a more "oops" 1 and said "I'm sorry I'm sorry. Sorry."

I say "they don't hurt anymore."

Kath says "I heard about it you got clobbered. Anyway sorry."

"Is that your sister?" Douglas says.

"Yeah" I say.

"You have a sister?" Gillian says.

"Yeah."

"How old is she?"

"12" I say.

"That's so cute" Gillian says.

"Oh right you don't have 1" Caroline says and she reaches into her purse and takes out a pack of Marlboro Lights cigarettes. I look around for The Mall security guards to come bust us and she lights 1 blows out the smoke and she crosses her legs and says "They're not so cute. They make little jokes about you smoking in front of your Mom they're always around in your face."

She took another puff a really long 1.

Gillian said "Like your Mom doesn't know you smoke. Besides she's a smokestack what's she going to say? She'll take a big long drag on her cigarette" and now Gillian imitates taking a big long drag on a cigarette "and she'll go "No Smoking"" she said this in a really deep voice then blew out the pretend smoke. Everybody starts laughing and I laugh too. "Can I have 1" Gillian said and Caroline pushes the cigarettes and the matches over to her and Gillian takes 1 out of the pack and lights it up. She looked different smoking than Caroline Caroline looks like a grown-up but sort of an old 1 like she was 30 or something and has been smoking since she was 1 Gillian sat up super straight and smoked more like "I'm smoking now".

"I don't smoke either" said Kath and she put her hand out and put it down on my arm I wasn't sure what to do but then she moved it.

"Oh my God so my Mom listen to what she did. She had a date last night with this lawyer guy so she buys this whole new outfit this really cute skirt and a silk Gianni [I'm not sure that's the right name] blouse and she's already getting ready when I get home at like 2:30 and she's running around yelling and smoking like non-stop and then she's finally ready at 6:00.

And she blows him off" said Caroline. She took a puff on her cigarette and looked upwards. "She calls him and cancels she says she's got a virus then of course she starts yelling at me I'm just like Mom."

"Your Mother is fucking insane" says Douglas.

"Hello you're telling me" Caroline says.

"My Mom has no identity as a woman" Gillian says.

She looks at me and I kind of nod.

"She used to be my Dads slave she did whatever he wanted cooking cleaning. Walking Lefty."

"Lefty?" I say.

"My dog."

"He used to be named Leif" Kath says.

"Oh shut up" Gillian says.

"After Leif Garrett" Kath says.

Gillian put her hand in front of her face.

"It's so awful. I was young I didn't know" she says.

"Leif" Kath says.

"So why can't anyone let me forget it?"

"Pretty much because we're talking about Leif Garrett" Caroline says flicking an ash right on the floor.

"You named your dog after Leif Garrett" Kath says.

"Well he's named Lefty now" Gillian says.

Caroline and Kath and even Douglas are laughing but I didn't know if Gillian thought it was funny or not.

"What kind of dog is he?" I asked her.

"He's a beagle" Gillian said.

"A beagle named Leif Garrett" Kath said and they all started laughing really hard.

I say "My sister's allergic to dogs so we can't have 1 but

when she leaves next year maybe we can get 1. Then I could take it to college with me or something."

"Where's she going?" said Gillian.

"College."

"I thought she's 12."

"That's my other sister this is the other 1. Beth."

"Oh. I was like who's this 12 year old girl that's going to college?"

"What's her name?" said Douglas.

"Beth Reskin."

"She goes to Hutch Falls?"

"Yeah."

"She's a senior?"

"Yeah."

Gillian said "Does she have black hair? And she wears Preppy sweaters?"

"That's her."

"Who does she hang out with?" Caroline asked.

"This girl Kathy. Not you" I said looking at Kath. Everyone laughed and I laughed too seeing where as these jokes just come out of me sometimes.

"Is anybody hungry?" said Caroline.

"I'm gonna get a Taco Salad" said Kath.

"Does anybody want a Chicken King?" said Gillian.

"Can I just have like the tomatoes from your Taco Salad?" Caroline asked Kath.

"I'm really tired of all the shit at The Mall" Douglas said.

"Are you getting anything?" Gillian asked me.

"I guess I'll get a Orange Julius."

They all looked at me.

"You eat disgusting food" said Gillian.

When everybody got up I thought about just blowing off the Orange Julius but then I got it. After everybody came back with all their food we just sat around talking about stuff. Then I saw Kaths watch and it was 10 minutes before 4:00 and I was meeting my Mom and Claire and Beth at 4:00 and in some sort of weird tribute I guess to my Dad we were meeting at Orange Julius. Especially after before with them knowing about my Mom making me lunch every day and all that I didn't want my whole family suddenly showing up like 1 of those really close families so I'm freaking out and Caroline starts digging around like crazy in her purse and then she says "I'm out." Everyone looked kind of worried. Gillian said "Let's just go" and everyone stood up and I stood up too. Gillian gave me this little wave and Caroline seemed too messed up because of not having cigarettes to say goodbye and Kath smiled and said "it was nice to meet you Jeremy I'm sure I'll see you again." And they all walked off into the mall and I stayed a little behind but Douglas was still there as we went by The Athletes Foot he said "those girls have to stop smoking. The problem is basic science smoke get lung cancer get lung cancer die." He shook his head and then without saying anything he went to the Exit. This left me with 5 minutes after all to walk around and then come back because thank God unlike me and my Dad the girls in my family never come anywhere early. Mr. Rasfenjohn said to "Spice things up" by saying exactly what I'm thinking about and using my imagination so here's what I was thinking about. (Mr. Rasfenjohn by the way isn't the most popular teacher because he's from Iran but I think he's cool and knows a lot about writing and the world and Iran and just how to be smart and philosophical in life.) Anyway I was thinking about that girl in The Limited I was thinking about what if she was coming towards me and just before we passed each other a bunch of guys from some other school came up and pushed her and said "Hey Bitch". Then 1 of them grabbed her Breasts. And then I went up and punched the guy who grabbed them in the face and he went flying and then I just looked at the rest of them and said "Not today guys." And they all looked at me and they couldn't decide what to do and then they picked their friend up from the ground and left. And me and her walked to the parking lot because I had to get her to her car safely and she said "thanks" and looked out the back window of her car as her mom drove her away at me. I don't always think about these things but sometimes I do. Then I thought about if instead we were still in The Limited and some psycho with a gun came in and said "Everyone Dies!" and started shooting the place up and she'd already left the aisle with the sweaters and gone to the back of the store and I got down on the ground and crawled through the aisles back to her and Claire wasn't there anymore so I didn't have to worry about her and just as I got to the back the psycho did too and just as he pointed his gun at her and was about to shoot I jumped up and grabbed the gun and we were both trying to get it and shots were going off into the ceiling and finally I got it and I didn't really mean to but we were still fighting and I shot him right in the middle of his forehead and blew his head off. And then I went up to her and she put her arms around me and she was crying so hard she couldn't say anything.

CHAPTER 6

HALLOWEEN

Now there's a big banner hanging from the ceiling in the Lunchroom with big smiling pumpkins all over it "Halloween Dance - Get Spooky". I'm not saying everyone's thinking about Halloween in fact people pretty much don't think about it at all because who really cares about Halloween but you know it's coming with the pumpkins.

Things are going OK with Renee I see her Monday Wednesday and Friday in Spanish and she definitely knows my name and sort of who I am—the guy in Spanish. 1 day we're sitting there and Mr. Eller announces "Dialogue Drill with the verb IR[1]." I suck at the verb IR because it doesn't sound like itself when you use it it's like "voy" and "vaya" and 2nd of all it doesn't even sound like a word. "IR." Versus say

1. To go.

"Comer"[2] which is Spanish for to eat but at least sounds like a word so anyway he says "Dialogue Drill with the verb IR" and me and Renee get partnered up and I go over and sit with her. "Hi Jeremy" she says. "Hey Renee" I say.

So then Mr. Eller announces "begin drill" and Renee usually goes 1st so I just wait she looks at the ceiling for a second then she says "Yo voy a la escuela."[3] I nod and I say "Si"[4] but like a question "Si?"[5] so that then she says "Si" because that makes it a dialogue. So she says "Si" and then it's my turn and before I forget how she conjugated the verb "IR" I say "Yo voy la casa"[6] (casa is pretty much my favorite word in Spanish because 1st of all it's easy to remember and 2nd of all unlike "IR" which when you use it doesn't sound like "IR" anymore casa always sounds like casa and 3rd of all because there's a restaurant "Mi Casa" which I've gone by about 10 million times). Anyway I say "Yo voy la casa" and Renee says "Si?" and I say "Si" but lately Mr. Eller expects us to say more even after we've had a dialogue and Renee looks at me and she says "Tu vas Halloween Dance?"[7]

I'm not sure for a second what she said but I think she's asking me if I'm going to the Halloween Dance and it turns out I'm right. So I say "Si" except then I realize I'm probably not going I just say Si because you pretty much say Si no mat-

---

2. To eat.
3. I go to the school.
4. Yes.
5. Yes?
6. I go to the house.
7. Are you going to the Halloween dance?

ter what anybody asks you and what if she's saying "Do you have a date for the Halloween Dance?" which I don't want to say no because then I seem like a loser but don't want to say "yes" because what if even though it's about the last thing that would ever happen even now that we're sort of Spanish friends she wants me to go with her so I say "I mean no". No is no in Spanish and English and Mr. Eller just came over and started to listen to us so I want to explain my "No" was the Spanish No and not the English no (even if the rest of my dialogue sentence was in English) and I say to Renee "I mean Si. No. Si." Like I'm insane. Mr. Eller is right over us and it turns out he heard the whole thing and he looks at Renee and says "Tu vas **A** la Halloween Dance."[8] Then he gets this mad look on his face with his eyes and everything and he says "I mean Tu vas a la Halloween Baila." And then Renee looks at me and repeats it (because he wasn't asking her he was telling her the right way to say it) and she says "Tu vas a la Halloween Baila" and I say "Si" and she says "Si?" and I say "Si".

Mr. Eller goes away to bother some other people and we sit there for a second and then I look at Renee sort of down in the middle but I'm not looking at her Tits and I say "Tu vas Halloween Dance?" she shrugs her shoulders and looks down at her notebook. I almost feel a little bit like I just asked her to go to the dance but I know there's more I'd have to say now like "Do you want to go?" but for 1 split millionth of a billionth of a millisecond I have the feeling like I might actually almost say it. Then the millisecond's over I look over at Juan

8. Are you going to the Halloween dance?

Ramirez on his poster Mr. Eller says "Termine Dialogue"[9] which means the dialogue is over.

The next couple days I'm walking around the halls and whenever I see Renee she looks sad she's looking down a lot and her face is just sort of stuck in the down position. I'm wondering about her and is it possible she doesn't have a date for the dance and that's what's wrong and it makes me kind of sad for her. I think about her a lot and how she is and does she like Hutch Falls or does she wish she was still in Japan and is she happy and sometimes I think I'm thinking about her more than I think about anything else. Because what else is there to think about all the time? I know Renee is nice to me in Spanish because she's that kind of a person or maybe she just thinks I'm nice and she likes me but sometimes when a person is a certain way you just know it means something like they could make you really happy or maybe vice versa but what isn't meant to be also isn't meant to be except in the alternate dimension where we don't live where everything's the opposite. Don't get the wrong idea I'm not going to kill myself for her like Romeo who I probably sound like but maybe I would if I had to. Like if she needed me to. But I know it's stupid. Anyway John McKnight who is basically obviously the guy who's going to take her to the dance hasn't said anything in the locker room or at soccer practice or anything I heard to Randy and I don't know who else would ask her but still people don't always mean what they say or they don't mean the way they look. So who knows?

Anyway something happened. The Halloween Dance was

9. End the dialogue.

Saturday and Wednesday I saw Gillian in the hallway by herself by the library. Nobody else was around we smile and wave whenever we pass each other ever since the day we had lunch and we do. I was wondering by the way if they were going to all eat with me again but they weren't in the Lunchroom that much I think they were always out smoking on the balcony and bringing their lunch and eating it there. It was either that or they snuck off campus to eat which I wouldn't be too surprised if they did or they didn't eat at all.

Anyway Gillian 1/2 stopped like when you're not sure if you're going to stop or not and said "Hi Jeremy."

"Hey" I said.

"How are you?"

"Good. What about you?"

"OK you know."

She sort of bounced around a little.

"We're going to the city this weekend" she said.

"Oh" I said.

"Saturday for The Halloween Parade."

"You're not going to the dance?" I said.

"No we're going into the city."

"Oh" I said.

"We'll probably go in the afternoon and then come back on the last train."

"Uh-huh" I said.

"If you're going all the way there you might as well stay late."

I nodded.

"So I'll call you" she said.

"OK" I said.

"When we know when."

"OK."

"I don't think I have your phone number."

I told her and she pulled the top off her pen with her mouth and wrote my number down sideways in huge letters on a whole piece of paper in her notebook.

The next few nights I was downstairs a lot because I wanted to be there when she called so I could get to the phone fast hopefully 1st but that was pretty much impossible with Beth and my Mom alive on this planet. But at least in time to keep them from getting it and asking who it is and especially Beth from the top of her lungs shouting "Jeeeere-myyyy" I just wanted to go to the phone fast like it was no big deal and just say hi.

She didn't call that night and she didn't call Thursday night I was going downstairs a lot and my Mom was starting to look at me like I was crazy she was sitting in the living room reading womens living room digest or something and wearing her blue jeans which my Dad never wore and when I went through 1 time she said "What ARE you doing?"

"Nothing" I said.

"You've been in and out of that KITCHEN 10 times in the last hour."

"I'm getting a dri"

"Are you sick?"

My Mom interrupts a lot.

"No."

"Do you feel alright?"

"I'm fine."

"Nothing's wrong?"

"Mom!"

"But you're going up and down the stairs so much."

Friday night we were eating dinner. Here's what dinner's like at my house. We eat in the dining room which is next to the living room all sitting at a rectangle shaped table in the middle of the room. We have matching placemats but every night the placemats are different because that's 1 of my Moms things I don't mean they're different every night because you get back to the same placemat you had about a month ago but they're different every night. Here are some of the things on them: Plants, fish, Big Ben from London with the rest of London behind it, famous paintings by famous painters like Vincent Van Gogh, and Rembrandt, Monkeys, the Bronx Zoo with a lot of animals, just their heads, flowers, The Age Of Radio with a picture of an old radio in the middle and then heads of old radio people around it in a circle like Jack Benny, NY Mets which Mom breaks out on my birthday even though I haven't liked baseball since I was about 10, Lizards Of The Nile, Lizards Of The SouthWest (I guess they had a Lizard sale), The Ten Commandments which sometimes in 1 of his funny moods my Dad points to the 1 about honoring your father and your mother and makes a face, Chinese Zodiac, Great Battles of World War II, Wine Growing Regions Of Northern France, Mickey Mouse and about a 100 others that she got on family trips and from kitchen stores. Anyway we're all sitting at our placemats and my Mom is serving dinner and you have to start eating because everything is according to her going to be totally ruined if it cools off even a little bit so we're about 1/2 way done by the time Mom finally gives a big very dramatic sigh and wipes her hands on a napkin and then sits down.

Then almost every night unless my Dad's totally exhausted we go around and tell about our day. Beth goes 1st. There used to be like a rule that you just talked about classes and what you studied that day or something you read or what my Dad called something "worthy of discussion" but about a year ago Beth had this kind of revolution where she started telling about her friends and stuff going on even with other kids that had nothing to do with her at all which my Dad didn't like but Mom put her foot down and Beth and Mom won. Not that my Dad is against friends. Just he likes stuff that's more serious for dinner table discussion. So from then on you could talk about anything you wanted and it even could be a little bit of a joke so I could say "I ate a pickle" or something and Dad didn't get so mad anymore. And Claire sometimes won't go.

OK so there we are and the phone rings. Beth when the phone rings I swear could get there before Bruce Jenner. It's not like she gets so many calls or anything but she likes to an-swer it even if it's for Mom or anybody else because then she knows what's going on and who's calling who and everything about everything about the phone.

But the thing is we're having Liver that night. You might think Liver is really gross but not my Moms. At soccer some-times the guys give each other shit and a lot of times it's about mothers like "Your Mother this and Your Mother that." 1 time Chris Halal said something to me that sort of implied my Mom has sex with every person on the soccer team and I said

"Your Mother can't even cook". Which I guess was kind of lame. But he didn't say anything else.

So anyway my Mom really can cook especially when she doesn't make fish I don't care what you say about her and probably her best thing of all is her Liver which isn't gross at all it's better I swear than the best steak and it's got this pepper sauce on it that's really great and onions which normally I don't like or not like all over the top and they just rock and when we have Liver my Dads mouth is practically watering and even Claire who doesn't even eat anything eats a lot and Beth has about 20 helpings the whole time she's trying to take more so nobody notices by sticking her fork out low at the Liver and looking over at something else when she forks it over to herself like then nobody'll notice. So the phone rings and Beth now is in this big Liver versus phone conflict which with other food you don't usually have because usually the phone always wins and in the 1 second she sits there not knowing what to do I start to get up but then before I'm even all the way up she's gone and through the living room like The Flash or more like Reverse Flash who's evil and in the kitchen I hear "Huh-low??????" with a big question mark at the end in this totally fake Beth voice and then there's a pause. And then of course Beth says "Who's calling pleeeese???" which she always does but with a different kind of like she doesn't quite believe it sound in her voice and then there's another pause and I know it's Gillian. I wait and there's this pause and then Beth comes in and really loud so whoever's on the phone can still hear looks at me and says "Jeremy it's Gillian!" like she's announcing the President of The United States is calling and I get up and go to the kitchen and the receiver is hanging there.

"Hello" I say.

"It's Gillian."

"Hey."

"Are you eating dinner?"

"No."

"OK. Well I wanted to tell you about the city we're meeting at the station at 3:00."

"3:00."

"Tomorrow."

"OK" I say.

"So you're coming?"

"Yeah."

"Oh. Great. I wasn't sure. OK. So" and there's this pause and I say "Yeah" again for some reason and then there's another pause and she says "I guess I'll see you at the station."

"Yeah" I say.

"OK then. Bye" she says.

"Later" I say.

She hangs up the phone and so do I.

I go back in the dining room and everybody's holding their forks up over their Liver like some kind of atom bomb just fell on Hutch Falls. And nobody's eating. Even my Dad. So they're looking at me and I just sit down and start to eat but of course Ms. Nosy Pain In The Ass says "Who's Gillian?"

"This friend of mine" I say.

"Is she that girl who wears black every day?" Beth says.

"No."

They're all still looking at me and finally I say "A bunch of us are going into the city."

"That's wonderful" my Mom says and she smiles this huge smile like good because I'm going places with people. "When are you going?" she says.

"Saturday."

"Halloween?" my Mom says and now she looks like I just said "The day they do human sacrifices of all the people from Hutch Falls."

"Yeah" I say.

She says "That's not a good idea. Can't you go another day?"

"No."

"Why not?"

"That's when we're going."

"But Jeremiah I don't like you being in New York at night and especially on Halloween with all those people running around in masks."

"People aren't more dangerous when they're wearing costumes" I say.

"You haven't been in New York on Halloween Jeremy."

"Have you?"

"No I don't go because it's not safe. I want you to go on another day."

"Mom it's the only" I start to say but she interrupts me again and says "There are 365 days in the year when you can go to New York but not on the 1 day when people are running around in masks."

"He'll be fine" my Dad suddenly says.

"Abe" my Mom says.

"Annie" my Dad says and that's it.

Before I fell asleep I sort of 1/2 thought 1/2 dreamed about what if we were all walking down the street in New York and a psycho-killer dressed as a skeleton tried to cut our throats with a switchblade but I hit him so hard I broke his bones right where they were on his costume too. I have pretty fast reflexes. Then I thought what if everybody's wearing a costume but me but I was sure Gillian would of said something if they were and they weren't the type of people who wear costumes anyway and neither was I.

The next day which is Saturday at 2:45 my Mom drops me off at the train and says to me as I get out "Just be careful OK?" and I say "OK" and I go up over the overpass to the other side where the trains to New York are. Gillian and everybody else wasn't there yet except for Kath.

"Hi Jeremy" she said.

She was wearing black pants and this shirt with long sleeves tucked out I think because of her being big and wanting to pretend she wasn't and she gave me a big smile. She had a plain face and black hair that was short. Now I was there with just her.

"Hey" I said. "Kath."

"You're 2nd" she said.

"Oh."

She turned around and looked down the track and she said "I really love New York".

"Yeah it's cool" I said.

"It really is" she said.

I looked at the parking lot but I didn't see anybody.

"Do you go a lot?" Kath said.

"I go to my Dads office sometimes or out to dinner."

"With your family?"

"I guess."

"What does your Dad do Jeremy?"

"He's a lawyer."

"My Mom hates New York she didn't even want me to go."

"Why?"

"She thinks everyone in New York is a pusher. She said to me "Don't go wandering around and don't talk to people."" She said this imitating her Moms voice. "Like everyone wants to kill you."

"You're old enough to take care of yourself."

"She's so paranoid."

"Why would everybody want to kill you?" I said.

"Some people want to kill you."

"Yeah" I said.

I didn't see them coming but Gillian and Caroline got there then and then right before the train came Douglas got there too. Caroline was dressed like usual but with a red ribbon in her hair maybe like a Preppy anti-Preppy statement I guess for Halloween and Gillian was dressed up a little in a really short skirt and skin colored panty hose and her usual red red lipstick. With her skirt I realized for the 1st time that she had legs. Douglas was even wearing these pretty nice pants and a very dark blue windbreaker it was kind of like everyone was all dressed up and I was glad Claire came in my room because I wasn't going to dress up at all but then Claire before I left came in and opened my bottom drawer which I didn't even know she knew what was in there and pulled out my special occasion corduroys which are blue and said "Definitely these." They looked good I thought with the light blue Alligator shirt with the green alligator I was wearing so I wore them and didn't take a jacket because it wasn't cold. (My Dad hates that alligator. He always says you're paying more for the alligator than the shirt). Later when I was about to go I went into Claires room and she was getting ready to go to her dance much later with Nell and she was dressed up in a dress made out of some kind of green felt or something she finally bought and I said "You look nice."

"Thanks" she said.

Anyway we got on the train and we went to 1 of those 4 seats across from each other and someone was going to have to sit in the 1 across the aisle alone and I figured it would be me because they were all friends but Douglas sat there and put his feet up on the chair across from him and leaned down like some kind of rebel who owned the train car. I sat across from Gillian and Kath sat next to me across from Caroline. Caroline had a Walkman which was pretty cool and she put it on as soon as the train left and started almost dancing in her seat to the music totally in her own little world all the way to New York and Gillian and Kath and Me talked some about nothing much and after a while we were in New York.

So here we were. Gillian was walking with her legs in her skirt which I couldn't help noticing but the rest of her wasn't as hot and Kath looked like she was thinking about something and Douglas was next to Gillian talking and Caroline's in a really good mood all of a sudden skipping even sometimes and spinning around in a circle like Mary Tyler Moore.

Anyway we walk a lot and finally we get to this place where

they're selling all kinds of stuff mostly jewelry and clothes on the street. It's all 60s stuff for hippies but the people selling it aren't hippies they're from India or someplace.

The girls are looking at stuff and me and Douglas are hanging out and I say "Girls would be happy if they spent their whole lifes shopping."

"Very True Statement" Douglas said.

"Yeah" I said.

"VTS."

"What?" I said.

"Very True Statement."

"Oh."

(That was the origin of VTS).

Anyway it must take us 2 hours to get down that fucking street with them stopping everywhere and trying on everything finally Gillian buys some earrings that hang down really far from her ears and look like they're from Ancient Egypt or Mesopotamia and Caroline buys and put on a brown metal bracelet with black designs in it and Kath doesn't buy anything even though she tried on a lot of things she said "I love it" about but then she always took whatever it was off and made kind of a "Well" face at it then put it back.

"Let's go" Caroline said when we left that street and she took off again. Later we were across the street from the World Trade Center which is a very famous building in New York. It's 2 extremely tall white rectangle shaped buildings right next to each other. There's nobody around except for a fountain and the whole thing looks like you're on Mars if Mars had 2 buildings on it. Caroline goes around to the back where there aren't any people either and it turns out there's another building I didn't know was back there there it's black and shorter and we're at the back of it and there's hardly any space between it and 1 of the huge white buildings. But there is a little so we go into this little space between the buildings which is about 10 feet wide and there's a staircase going down and Caroline goes about 1/2 way down and sits down on the stairs. So do we. It's not at all totally dark yet and I just sort of know why Caroline took us here. It's really cool. We're all sitting there and Caroline says "Look" and she's looking up so I look up and you can see straight up between the building and the other building and even though the black 1s not as tall it's still very tall and they're both right next to you so you just feel like you're in Star Wars or something plus the sky which you only see this 1 piece of inbetween the 2 buildings at the top is a shape of sky you don't see too much or ever and it's weird because it's just about the opposite but it makes me think of the super huge sky in The Grand Teton National Park and then Caroline says "It's like a tunnel. But going up." Nobody said anything and then she said "it's so cool." And it was.

We just sat there sometimes looking up. Gillian was sitting on the stair right over me and Douglas was in the middle of the stairs and Caroline was on the other side and so was Kath. When we were out there Caroline was singing Pink Floyd out loud.

WE DON'T NEED NO EDUCATION
WE DON'T NEED NO THOUGHT CONTROL
I DON'T KNOW THIS LINE
TEACHER LEAVE THOSE KIDS ALONE

This is so what Caroline types like because it's so Fuck You to everybody. I prefer better songs. Like 2 Out Of 3 Ain't Bad by Meatloaf which goes:

I WANT YOU I NEED YOU BUT THERE AIN'T NO WAY
   I'M EVER GONNA LOVE YOU
NOW DON'T BE SAD CAUSE 2 OUT OF 3 AIN'T BAD

We can as human beings all understand and relate to a relationship where the guy really likes the woman and wants her and needs her but just doesn't feel she's the 1 for him for all time.

Anyway it was getting pretty dark now and also a little cold. We rode the Subway into The Village where the big Halloween Parade was it was cool wandering around there it was night and there were a lot of college students and older people and people from every country. Older guys checked out Caroline a lot a few times they even said things like "Hey" and she'd give them a little "Hi - eat shit" smile and keep going I think it was because of her black stockings and her I'm a slut look and everything.

We ate dinner at a restaurant. Me and Douglas feasted on burgers and fries with BBQ Sauce and milk shakes and Kath sat eating a salad. I don't remember what Gillian and Caroline ate.

Kath said "Where is that weird soccer Coach from?"

"Romania" I said.

"What the fucks he doing in Hutch Falls?" Douglas said.

"He come to theees cuntry for beeetr soccer life" I said and it sounded a lot like Coach Kurlyesku even more than I thought it would and everybody laughed.

Here's the bad thing that happened. It was getting pretty late and the streets were filling up with people in costumes after dinner. The costumes were not like a Pirate or Ghost. People were dressed up as things you would never in a million years think of to dress up as like a carrot and a vacuum cleaner and a giant Tit. We were walking down this 1 street and then through these smaller streets and it was getting later and crowded. Caroline was smoking non-stop and Gillian smoked too I thought about smoking a cigarette but I decided not to. If my Dad found out (by smelling me or something) our house would cave in not with him yelling and screaming like some parents but with 1 of my Dads patented "Why do you think you did that" conversations with me where I never have a reason why I did it so I always end up being like "I don't know" and he proves that's why I shouldn't of done it. Smoking though is a especially especially heinous crime and is probably the 1 thing you can get sent to reform school for in my family. And I didn't want to smoke anyway.

Anyway people were going to this 1 street where the Parade was and you could tell the Parade was starting so we went over to the street and found a spot to stand in. Right after we got there the street suddenly got filled up totally with people in costumes marching some of them were in big groups of 20 people or more all dressed up 1/2 naked as Indians or something and then some people were alone with other people. There was The Lone Ranger with his horse and 2 people dressed up as gay guys holding hands. Everybody was screaming and making tons of noise. Some people were playing kazoos and violins and instruments. A group of men dressed up as women went by marching they were wearing dresses and they had a big float with basically a big Dick coming out of it skin colored and very realistic and they all had girls hairdos and lipstick on their lips. They were waving to the crowd and laughing and everybody was cheering a lot. Douglas was right next to me.

"Fags" I said.

"What?" he said.

"Fags" I said.

"Do you have some kind of problem with Fags?" Douglas said.

"No" I said.

"So why do you call them that?"

"I don't know."

Douglas turned around and left. I stood there for a second. I didn't see the girls and I didn't know where anybody was and I wondered if they'd go back without me. I wished I didn't say Fag even though I didn't know why it pissed him off so much everybody said it in the locker room all the time and it never bothered people.

I turned around and walked into the crowd. I saw Gillian leaning on a building made of brick with a cigarette and talking to Kath. You could tell they were talking about something important and that that important thing was probably me. A little over from them Caroline was sitting down on the sidewalk and she wasn't smoking and Douglas was standing there I wanted to go over to Gillian and Kath but I was worried about Douglas being right there so I didn't go over until Gillian saw me and once she did I had to go over but I went to the side of them further away from Douglas. When I got there Douglas walked around the corner and Caroline got up and followed him.

"Jeremy what happened?" Gillian said.

"I don't know."

"Douglas is really sensitive" Kath said.

"What'd you say?" Gillian said.

"I don't know" I said.

"Well did something happen?" Gillian said.

"I think I said "Fag"" I said.

"Oh" said Gillian.

She took a worried puff on her cigarette.

"I don't have anything against them" I said.

"I know" said Gillian.

I just stood there.

"He really really doesn't like that" she said.

"Is he into that or whatever?" I said.

Gillian said "No. He's just sensitive about people."

"Oh" I said.

"Drama drama drama" Kath said.

"It's OK" Gillian said.

"Is he staying with you tonight?" Kath said to Gillian.

"I don't know."

I didn't know he was staying over at Gillians but I knew they weren't involved or anything it was just as friends.

Finally Caroline and Douglas came back and it was late now so we head to the train station. Later on the train Douglas commented on my jock mentality. Caroline was saying that the guys who made passes at her on the street were so gross and Douglas said "It's the jock mentality. It breeds ignorance" and he looked at me.

That night I went into Claires room. She was in her red pajamas with Chinese letters on them sitting at her desk writing in her diary.

"What're you writing?"

"About the dance."

We looked at each other for a minute and I thought about asking her about the whole Fag thing but I didn't think she knew much about Douglas and what he was like and stuff so I said "Goodnight" and went back to my room and my day ended with me turning the radio on to WMRQ and "Night Love" was on which is like "WMRQ with Night Luuuuv" and a song called I'm All Out Of Love (by Air Supply) was on which goes

I'M LYING ALONE WITH MY HEAD ON THE PHONE
    THINKING OF YOU TIL IT HURTS
I KNOW YOU HURT TOO BUT WHAT ELSE CAN WE
    DO TORMENTED AND TORN APART
I WISH I COULD CARRY YOUR SMILE IN MY HEART
    FOR TIMES WHEN MY LIFE SEEMS SO LOW
IT WOULD MAKE ME BELIEVE WHAT TOMORROW
    COULD BRING WHEN TODAY DOESN'T REALLY
    KNOW
DOESN'T REALLY KNOW

Then it goes

I'M ALL OUT OF LOVE
I'M SO LOST WITHOUT YOU

I KNOW YOU WERE RIGHT BELIEVING FOR SO LONG
I'M ALL OUT OF LOVE
WHAT AM I WITHOUT YOU
I CAN'T BE TOO LATE TO SAY THAT I WAS SO WRONG

When I hear this I think about Renee because this is to tell the truth how I feel about her except for the part about her hurting too and being torn apart and us not talking on the phone. After that song when I was waiting to fall asleep which I do with the radio on I thought about Douglas and who he was and if I liked him or not and the big Tit and all the guys saying Hi to Caroline and I pictured all the men dressed up as women and how fucking weird that stuff was and then I guess I fell asleep wondering about the world like why do we dress up in costumes. And why do we have parades. These are specific times when everybody decides to scream and yell and be happy and have fun. Why don't we just have fun all the time? I don't know. I guess it's culture.

CHAPTER 7

GILLIANS BASEMENT

I'm sitting in Gillians basement with Gillian. It's a long story how we got there. After we went to New York Gillian saw me in the hall and invited me to go out to the balcony where they smoke and eat lunch. I said I didn't bring my lunch that day and she said to buy lunch in the Lunchroom and I said you can't take trays out of the Lunchroom and she just sort of looked at me like "Well you could probably get away with it". So I went.

The balcony is on the 2nd Floor at the back of the Main Building over the Maintenance Yard. The Maintenance Yard has a fence around it so no one can see you up there unless they're really trying to. You have to go through this green door to get there and so I go through and they're sitting out there and Caroline and Gillian are smoking I sit down against the railing where Douglas is too. It's weird being there and I'm eating a hamburger with no fries and they're talking then the door opens and Mr. Caddup the Painting and Drawing teacher who I've never had walks out. I start to freak out my Dad would pretty much kill me for being out there with people smoking and you can get suspended for smoking in school which I never even came close to before and Mr. Caddup goes to the end of the balcony and then he lights up a cigarette. "He bummed 1 from me once" Gillian leans over whispering to me.

OK! So anyway Douglas was his usual kind of serious bummed out self but he said hi and the whole Fag thing was no big deal anymore and then Gillian invited me out there again the next week and pretty soon I was going every couple days. Then 1 time we're out there and I'm eating the worlds most disgusting pizza from the Lunchroom which I swear is wet like it got rained on and Gillian just says "Do you want to come over tonight and watch Space 2000" which is a big special about these people who get trapped in a corner of the Galaxy and discover this new world.

I have no idea these guys like that kind of stuff which I definitely want to watch because I enjoy Science Fiction except it's the 1st Knicks game of the season that night. "You guys are watching Space 2000?"

"Not me" says Caroline.

"Boring" says Kath.

Gillian says "Just me and Douglas but everyone's coming."

"Cool." Even though I want to watch the game but I want to watch Space 2000 too.

So we're in Gillians basement. Gillians basement has 2 couches next to each other at about a 90 Degree angle and bean bag chairs 1 red and 1 green and a super-thick rug like my Dad won't let my Mom get because it traps odors and a bar with a big mirror behind it and chairs which both of my parents don't want in our basement. Gillians mother comes down and asks if we don't want anything to eat or drink and I'm starving but I don't say it but fortunately Douglas says "OK" and she comes down with a tray full of Fried Chicken and mashed potatoes and salad and Coke. The salad wasn't too popular except for Caroline. Space 2000 was stupid during 1 commercial I said I wanted to see the score of the Knicks game and they let me switch channels and Reggie Carter who's my favorite player and never gets in was in I saw him make this sweet pass to Richardson who passed to Cartwright who dunked but it was Carter who set it up and they weren't even like "Nice pass Reggie". The other players aren't I don't think nice to him I don't know why. Anyway after Space 2000 Caroline and Kath were already bored and went somewhere I don't know where and Douglas suddenly left and Gillian and me are down there alone and we go upstairs to see her room. Her room is basically a bed and a desk but it's normal it's not all pink or anything like a major girls room except for her closet where the door is covered so much you can't even see any door at all with cut-outs from magazines and pictures and stuff that say: PEACE STYLE HIPPIES ROMANTIC THE NEW FRONTIER LIFESTYLES BILLIE JEAN KING LOVE OPERA TRUTH JUNKIES WILD. It's also messy there's books and magazines and junk on the floor and also she's got so many candles all over the place (they're not lit) I wonder if she's going to burn her room down.

We sit down on the floor me leaning on the bed and her not.

Gillian says to me "So did you score a goal or something last week?"

"No" I say.

"Douglas said he heard you scored a goal."

"No" I say.

What happened was at the end of the game with the score tied 1-1 I slide-tackled this guy Jock Dumont who grew up in France and is really good because about all they do in France from the time they're born is play soccer and the ball went into the goalpost and bounced off and went over my head and then somehow Jock got his foot up super fast as lightning and the ball hit it and bounced off and just zoomed right into the goal. Let me tell you by the way whatever you've heard about it time doesn't go in slow motion. Time goes faster when something like that happens. Also we were 7 and 8 before that game and Randy gave a speech in the locker room before the game where he was practically crying about getting to .500 and being competitive and pride and dignity.

Anyway there was a pause and then I said "I slide-tackled a guy and the ball went off the goalpost and this guy kicked it in."

"That's great" said Gillian.

"No it was our goal" I said.

"Oh."

Gillian leaned down to stretch and she was wearing this shirt the same color as lemonade that went down under her neck and 1 of the straps of her bra was out instead of under the shirt anyway and then when she leaned over to stretch the part of the shirt under her neck came out a lot and I saw down into her shirt where I saw her whole bra and it was pretty much flat against her with nothing in it. Then she sat up and smiled like she was nice and stretched out now and I watched her lips and her lipstick and they would have been really great lips on somebody else and she was probably the 1st person where I ever even noticed her lips because I was more into Breasts and faces.

So then she says "Were you ever in love Jeremy?"

"It depends on what you mean by love" I say.

Gillian says "really in love. Where you'll do anything for someone. Where you'll die for them where they are the single most important thing in your life and nothing else even comes close and you think about them all the time."

If Gillian could read minds right then she'd see a big picture of me sitting next to Renee in Spanish. That's real. Then there's also a picture of me and Renee sitting next to each other on a couch somewhere with our sides touching and not only now but when we're older too. This is more than lust or just sex because I really believe in Renee as a person. I say "I don't know. Maybe once or twice but I'm not sure it's your definition. Have you?"

Gillian looks at me and puts her hands and arms around her legs.

"There was a boy when we lived in Massachusetts he lived down the street from us and we walked to school together every day. We kissed and stuff. I loved him so much but we were so young it was 6th Grade so I don't know."

She stopped talking then started again.

"Kath gets crushes but that's obviously different she talks and talks about some guy and how great he is and then she gets depressed when he doesn't ask her out even though she doesn't even know him."

"Uh-huh" I say.

"Douglas I'm not sure about. There is 1 girl you know her. But I don't know if he's "in love" with her."

"Mmm-hmm" I say.

"Caroline I'm positive is not in love. With the guy she's going out with."

"Oh" I said.

"You knew she had a boyfriend right?"

"Yeah. I mean I thought she did."

"Ritchie. He was going to meet us in New York but he didn't come he sells real estate."

"How old is he?" I said.

"23."

"23?" I said.

"He's a jerk. He's just going to hurt her and he's a pervert for going out with a girl in High School but she likes older guys that's all she goes out with."

"I don't get that I mean people should go out with people their own age" I said.

"A little older is OK" said Gillian.

"Yeah. But not that older."

"Sometimes I think Douglas has a thing for her" Gillian said.

"For who?"

"You know."

"Caroline?"

"Not that he's in love with her but I have a feeling about it. Call it womens intuition."

"My sisters have that" I say.

"All women have it."

"Really?"

"Yes. I've got intuitions about everybody."

"Really?"

"Uh-huh. I've got intuitions about you."

"Yeah?" I said.

"Uh-huh."

There was a pause for a second.

"Like what?" I said.

"I think you're a very passionate person."

"Mmm-hmm."

"And when you fall in love it will be very intense."

"I guess I'm like that" I said.

"Caroline thinks love is having some guy think you're great and tell you how great you are all the time and buy you flowers and then treat you badly as long as he worships you but that's not love."

"Yeah" I said.

"But she's had a hard time."

She was sitting sideways next to the bed. I waited a second then I said "Was it tough when your parents got divorced?"

"Yes. They were like 1 person. My Mom has no identity without my Dad."

"Oh" I said. "Divorce is sort of wrecking our country."

"Do you think?"

"Definitely. It's very damaging to kids. They don't have any permanent things in their lifes with divorce. So they're confused."

Gillian bit her lips which she does.

"If you were married would you ever cheat on your wife?" she said.

"No. It's the worst thing a man can do to a woman. It's disrespectful. Totally. It destroys a persons self-confidence in themself. Would you?"

"I wouldn't try to. I'd try to work things out but if I fell out of love everything would change I can't live without love."

"You could leave him."

"I suppose that's true."

We were quiet for a minute then I said "You're from Massachusetts?"

"Yes."

We went back downstairs and Douglas was there in the red bean bag chair Gillian said "Are you staying" and Douglas said "Yes" and then he said to me "You can't get a decent nights sleep at my house." That was weird and it reminded me of before on Halloween when Kath asked Gillian if he was staying there so I guess he does a lot because for some reason he can't get a decent nights sleep at his house. In a lecture this professor came and gave on the modern family in Sociology I learned that could be because he lives in an area with a lot of gunfire or his parents are addicted to cocaine or ruthlessly beat him. But probably he just can't sleep or something. Anyway we had some more chicken. Caroline and Kath never came back. It was cool to be out on a Friday night even if we were in watching TV and drinking Cokes and eating at Gillians house.

CHAPTER 8

THE BANANA MALOOSA FIASCO

In the upper reaches of lower Nigeria lives a tribe of indigenous African natives called the Ife. The Ife live a simple pastoral life of farming and fishing and just hanging around a lot. Sometimes they have big fires in the middle of their village and have traditional dances and feasts. This is where they often eat The Banana Maloosa.

The Banana Maloosa plays an important role in my life because of Miss Solovoy who is my World History teacher. She's short and I guess you could say she's about 40 or 50. She's famous for saying "What do you think a window is?" to Alan Binelow when he broke a window with his World History book trying to squash a bee on the window and the book and all the glass and I guess the bee went crashing down onto the courtyard below where fortunately no one was walking to the football field or anything.

Anyway Miss Solovoy always tries to inspire us. Her most recent attempt was right before Thanksgiving when we were doing a World Cultures Segment and in honor of Thanksgiving she assigned us to study celebrations around the world in particular we had to do reports presenting celebrations meaning we had to actually do the celebration for our report. And when we picked assignments I wasn't really paying attention and before I knew it I got the only 1 left which was The Banana Maloosa.

To be more direct it's not like my actual assignment was "Cook the Banana Maloosa" it was actually "Cuisine Of The Ife Tribe Of Nigeria". In our unit on African Tribal culture we didn't study the Ife in particular so the 1st thing I did was go to the library I looked up the Ife in the encyclopedia but even though it told a lot about them the food part only talked about how they hunted and ate Hippopotamus meat they killed and cooked in a special oven made out of dirt. I wasn't going to be cooking any Hippopotamus in an oven made out of dirt so the next thing I did was go to the librarian Mrs. Spendel who found me a cookbook on dishes from around the world called Dishes From Around The World. Some of the dishes in The Table Of Contents include:

Sahara Water Crusts	p. 7
Hunter's Portion	p. 10
Andean Twice-Smoked Bigara Root	p. 19
The Banana Maloosa	p. 28
Tahiti Earth Bounty Salad	p. 31
Hmong Chicken Fritters	p. 32

Hyena Stew (we don't have a lot of Hyenas
   in N.J.)   p. 40
Chinese Rice   p. 46

And many other things. So I look up a bunch of stuff and when I got to The Banana Maloosa even though it didn't say anything about the Ife in particular it did say it was eaten by many tribes of Western Africa and that's where the Ife live.

Here is what it said:

THE BANANA MALOOSA IS A TRADITIONAL FESTI-VAL DISH OF MANY INDIGENOUS TRIBES OF WEST-ERN AFRICA. RELYING HEAVILY ON THE USE OF BANANAS, A STAPLE ITEM WHICH GROWS ABUN-DANTLY IN THE REGION'S SEMI-TROPICAL CLIMATE, THIS DISH IS COOKED AND THEN BURIED IN THE GROUND FOR 3 DAYS BEFORE BEING EATEN. IT IS SERVED AT FESTIVALS CELEBRATING THE HARVEST AND MARKING PUBERTY RITES. BECAUSE ALL INGRE-DIENTS MAY NOT BE AVAILABLE IN LOCAL MARKETS, SUBSTITUTES ARE GIVEN IN PARENTHESES.

I xeroxd the recipe and took it home for my Mom to cook. My Mom kind of squinted her eyes when she looked at the recipe.

"I don't know about this" she said.

"Why" I said.

"It doesn't look very good."

"It's my assignment I have to make it."

"Alright then we'll see what happens."

At the grocery store I went down the list while my Mom shopped for other stuff:

22 Green Bananas
2 Cups Salt
2 Quarts Whole Milk
4 Table Spoons Ground African Fern Bark (Substitute Salt)
1 Stick Butter

I tossed some Corn Pops in the cart because usually my Mom didn't get sweet cereals because my Dad didn't believe in them and I got some Snack Pack too because if my Dad knew Snack Pack existed he wouldn't believe in it but mostly I got the ingredients.

That night I helped my Mom cook The Banana Maloosa. Let me assure you mashing 22 green bananas is not as easy as it sounds. And then putting the salt and the milk and the extra salt in is no big deal but to get the butter in you practically have to remash the whole thing.

Finally we flattened it down low in the pan. It was yellow and flat and about 3 inches high. When I told Mom time was up 1 hour later she took it out of the oven and it looked about the same as when we put it in except it was a little brown. It smelled like bananas.

"We should of made an extra 1 so we could taste it" my Mom said.

We left it in the pan and wrapped it in saran wrap and Moms usual 5 pounds of tin foil and we put it in the fridge. The next morning I took it out and got all the paper plates and plastic forks and knives and napkins I bought at the store and took it to school.

World History was 3rd Period before lunch. I was lugging the Banana Maloosa around with me all morning because it didn't fit in my locker so I was psyched it was finally time. Lenea Vovich was in World History with me and she sat in the front row right where she was looking at whoever was giving a report her black haircut was long and feathered and from the back it moved side to side whenever she moved her head even a little I don't know why but it made me think of a bird. Also she would probably tell Renee everything that happened if anything happened. Also John McKnight is in the class but he didn't sit with her even though he could he sat in the 2nd row with some other guys who weren't his best friends but were in the class like Billy Culom and Henry Stem who plays baseball with him. In the back row with me usually was Leslie Galata and Frank Taganyika who was Japanese who were friends with each other and people like that who aren't even all worth mentioning.

Anyway there are 2 reports before me Mating Dances Of The South American Tenge Tribe which is hard to explain except Alice Lipinski and Janey Drew who did it giggled the whole time but still I give them credit because they did do it and did dance in a mating way in front of the whole class and God Songs Of The Indonesian Turtuit People which sounded kind of like Billy Joel with really weird words. I was the last 1 and when I got up I guess I was very nervous everyone was staring at me so I just started. I still have my note cards and here's what I said:

"In Nigeria live a tribe of indigenous Africans known as the

Ife. The Ife have lived in Nigeria for many centuries living according to very old tribal ways and customs. They have been effected by modern civilization. 1 of the important parts of Ife society is eating. In addition to wild game which they hunt and kill and some fishing and some farming of grains the Ife have special festivals like puberty and harvest festivals when they eat special foods. 1 such food is The Banana Maloosa. The Banana Maloosa is made out of bananas which are plentiful in the forested regions where the Ife live and are therefore a staple product. For my report I have made a Banana Maloosa."

I put my note cards down and started to unwrap The Banana Maloosa which was on Miss Solovoys desk. Everyone was trying to see it and when it was uncovered I opened the plates and forks and knives and napkins Miss Solovoy took them and started to pass them around. I picked up the knife I brought from our kitchen. I wasn't sure how to cut it there were 30 people in the class and enough Banana Maloosa for everyone to have 1 small to medium size piece. I started cutting the Banana Maloosa which was a little harder to cut than I expected. Then I got out the 1st piece which was hard and after that it was still hard to cut but easier to get the pieces out and a few minutes later everyone had a piece of Banana Maloosa in front of them and a knife and a fork and a napkin.

I'm not sure why but everybody waited and then finally Miss Solovoy who was sitting next to where I was standing next to the desk said "OK everybody."

Everybody dug in with their fork but not much happened so they picked up their knife and started cutting. Finally everybody took a bite. Nobody immediately threw up or anything. But people weren't exactly smacking their lips or going "Mmm Mmm Good" either. In fact people were chewing really really slow and nobody said anything. Miss Solovoy coughed a little.

I started to chew. The Banana Maloosa didn't really taste like bananas it was super chewy almost like having a huge huge piece of gum in your mouth and it sort of had no flavor at all. Except then once you swallowed it it did taste like bananas. But sort of like really old really gross salty bananas.

If this was 7th Grade or even 8th a lot of the guys would of been like "Eeew gross" and "Am I supposed to eat this?" and "Nice going Jeremy" but now they're more mature and everyone is just totally quiet. I still have a bite of Banana Maloosa in my mouth and I don't know what to do because even I don't want to swallow it and Miss Solovoy didn't say anything and it may sound wimpy and pathetic but to tell the entire total truth my eyes got that watery feeling you get sometimes.

Finally Miss Solovoy turns to Arthur Deam who is 1 of the black people in the class. There are 2 sections the smart black kids and the goofing off black kids and they don't sit together. The goofing off black kids don't actually goof off they usually more just sort of sit there I sit there sometimes too so I'm not saying it's because they're black just that that's who they are. Anyway Arthur is 1 of the goofing off ones and Miss Solovoy says "Arthur what do you think?" he doesn't answer and suddenly everybody I can tell is thinking the same thing which is she's asking him because The Banana Maloosa is from Africa. And he's black so he is too. Which I don't think she was because Miss Solovoy asks that question to somebody after every report to stimulate conversation and this time it just happened to be Arthur but still I think everyones thinking it and Miss Solovoy is too because I'm right next to her and I hear her say "oh" quietly. Then Arthur says "I don't know" and there's this silence again where you can't tell if Arthur's thinking it or not because a lot of times he'll say "I don't know" and then suddenly John McKnight says "I think The Ife need to get a McDonalds." A bunch of people laughed and then Mike Potter the class clown-comedian says "Yeah we should open a McDonalds in Nigeria" and everybody including Miss Solovoy laughs and then Mike says "We could sell Big Ifes" and everyone laughs more and then somebody else says "And Ife Fries" which wasn't even funny but now no matter what anybody says we all just laugh more. Then I put the tin foil and saran wrap and extra plates and forks in the Banana Maloosa pan and I go back to my seat.

After school was over I went home and hung out and had dinner. Then I called Gillian. She'd called me 3 times and once we talked for over 2 hours and once I wasn't home and called her back so I was used to calling her. We have an office in the back of the house next to the garage where my Mom goes sometimes to do volunteer work and where once in a while my Dad goes for some peace and quiet there's a typewriter and a phone there so that's where I go for private conversations. Beth has a phone in her room so she doesn't have to which is not totally unfair because she didn't get it until she was a Junior. Anyway I call and Gillians mom answers and gets Gillian. I say hi and she starts talking about all the million typical things girls like to talk about including: what happened in every 1 of her classes, who said something smart, who said something stupid, what her mom said when she got home, what her mom meant when she said what she said when she got home, and what she thought about just about everyone in the world. I say "Uh-huh." Then I said "So I did that Banana Maloosa thing today."

"So how was it?" she said like she was really excited.

"Bad. Way too salty" I said.

"Oh no" she said like she was really sad.

"Yeah I pretty much poisoned everybody. It was funny though."

"Funny?"

"People were like "Those Ife need a McDonalds.""

"Well I don't think that's so funny" Gillian said.

"What?"

"Everybody's always making fun of everybody."

"It was funny" I said.

"I don't think it's funny. You worked very hard on that report and you cooked The Banana Maloosa and it didn't go well."

"Um" I said.

"I don't suppose somebody could just eat something and not make somebody else feel bad about it?"

I said "But you couldn't eat it. It was uneatable."

"Oh I don't know people are so - so - something."

"I didn't even eat it."

I realized Gillian was really sensitive.

"I wish it wasn't so salty" I said.

Then Gillian asked me how Carter did in the Knicks Game and I said 3 minutes no points no rebounds 1 assist. The truth was after the game which was the night before I thought for a long time about Richardson breaking his ankle and Williams injuring his eye and both of them sitting out the rest of the season and Carter leading the Knicks to the Finals and then winning it all and Richardson and Williams on the bench just watching and then when it's over both coming up to Carter and giving him a big hug while he cried a little happily and saying "Good job man" and Williams saying to the newscaster "That's my boy."

Anyway we said good night I went back through the living room to go upstairs and my Dad was reading the paper in his chair and he said "You too?" which meant now I talked on the phone all the time like Claire and Beth and my Mom. I said "No." Then I went upstairs.

CHAPTER 9

GILLIANS BASEMENT PART II

Gillians basement was sort of unfancy probably because her parents are divorced. Her Mom works at some kind of organization but that probably doesn't pay enough to remodel a basement which can be a very expensive proposition. In fact my Mom tried to get my Dad to remodel our basement for a long time and he always said it was too expensive and a waste of money until he said OK. At Gillians some things like the carpet and the couches were old and 1 of the bean bag chairs had a hole and leaked bean stuffing all over the place. The TV was OK. It smelled like an old basement. I liked going down there there was this feeling down there like you never knew what was going to happen.

Gillians Mom respected her privacy too so we could be down there and have privacy. Gillians Mom wasn't crazy. She was a little strange but she wasn't mean so it wasn't like having a mother who beat you or something and destroyed your sense of yourself. Her father lived 4 miles away.

Anyway we're down in the basement with everybody and Kath who wasn't around as much as the rest of us because she's sick or doesn't feel like going out. It's Saturday night and Gillians Mom isn't home but might be coming home soon. Caroline by the way was wearing leather pants which I've never seen her wear and Kath is in sweats because she likes to be comfortable and I don't wear Alligator shirts when I go out at night anymore so I've got a very soft brown sweater my Mom got me last year on and of course my trusty soccer jacket which I'm not wearing. We're talking about sex we're speculating about who in the class had it and joking about who obviously hasn't had it. Douglas and Kath haven't either and Gillian never told me if she ever did but she hasn't had a boyfriend since I've known her which was over a couple months now and as for Caroline who knows even though we all kind of assume probably. Anyway we start talking about how guys always want to have sex but girls are more into love and emotions and maybe more grown-up which is Gillians opinion and then Caroline says "I don't think you should live with somebody. No really I don't I don't believe in sex before marriage."

"Oh please" says Kath because we all know Caroline does a lot even though no one unless Gillian and Kath and they're not telling knows exactly how far she's gone but we know she must at least believe in it I guess because of everything about her. Caroline says "I don't I think you should wait. Because it's like well you just delve into stuff you're not ready for. Guys too." She makes this face like "So there" the way she does when she's got an idea she's going to believe no matter what.

"Yeah well. Okay fine who here has had sex?" Caroline says.

Nobody says anything.

"Jeremy?" she says.

I say "Well I don't know exactly what you mean by sex but"

"Douglas?" Caroline says.

"I'm waiting for my wedding night" he says. Everybody laughs. Then he says "I'm on a quest for my true love."

"Oh please" says Kath. She's rolling her eyes.

"Douglas is right it's a completely different experience when you're in love" says Gillian.

"It's a feeling you get" Gillian says next.

"People don't even know when they're in love. Not for sure. Everybody's just guessing. Even married people" I say.

"Do you think?" said Kath.

"Yeah" I say.

We were sitting on the floor and after everybody was quiet for a second Caroline said "Douglas give me a backrub." Douglas got off the other couch from the 1 I was on and sat behind Caroline and put his hands on her and started to rub. We all watched for a minute then Kath said "I'll do you" to me she got off the couch and sat down in front of it and leaned back against it and I got off the couch and moved down in front of her and I sat there wondering how far back to sit because I didn't want to crush her tits. Her tits are really big in the way big girls tits are not so much so they're great but just so they're big like as part of the fatness. Which is still big but you can tell squishy. She put her hands on my shoulders and she starts to rub and then she says "Relax" which is like announcing with a megaphone to the whole world "Jeremy's not relaxed" and which makes you more unrelaxed and then Gillian sat down in front of me and said "do me." She was wearing a blue wooly shirt with these little holes you could almost see through and with 2 bra straps pressing through it on her shoulders I put my hands on her shoulders with my fingers kind of spread out so I wasn't right over her bra and I started to rub I was trying not to touch the bra which is hard when you're trying to rub somebodys back until I moved my hands farther out and squeezed there and then moved back inbetween the bra straps and her neck with my hands and squeezed there. That was when I noticed there were all these tiny little see-through hairs on her neck. They were the smallest little hairs I ever saw. They weren't bad like being hairy. They were more like on a fish or something just some thing you never saw that then you see. Kath is squeezing my shoulders but it didn't feel especially anything. Meanwhile Douglas's about 2 feet away doing Caroline and her leather pants are sticking out straight in front of her on the floor and I swear she starts moaning like "Uuuuh" and "Mmmmm" like she's fucking or something and Douglas's got his usual bored look on his face but I'm not buying it for a second I'm sure he's faking it to be cool and I can see Carolines Tits which are pointy like some girls are and don't really go out to the sides at all but still go forward with their pointiness so that I definitely crave them. And Kath is moving down now and rubbing my back lower so I do the same thing to Gillian and when I move down I realize for the 1st time her back is super super thin and I can feel all her bones and her spine which is sticking out and I press around the bones and she moves a little and I'm looking over at Douglas and I'm thinking he's there with his hands all over Caroline and I'm stuck here I think between the fat and the flat even though it's mean to think and even though I'm not really into Caroline like for sex like I am totally with Renee still I think he's pretty lucky and I'm not having too much fun or luck. Gillian is bending her head way down and Kath is breathing all over my neck and suddenly I get an idea and I move my hands up and start doing Gillians head which feels weird like having someones head in your hands. For a second I pretend it's Renee and her head and that makes me feel bad because it's Gillians head but still I do. Something pretty intense happened about a week before with Renee even though she didn't know it. We had our last soccer game of the season versus RTS (Rianeck Township High). Our season has kind of gone down the drain at this point because we're 8-15. Fan support has dwindled considerably. So it was the last game of the season and nobody even cared and especially since it was away nobody came. At 1/2 time I was disgusted with us and our effort and how much we lost all year and losing again and again and again and I went to the visitors locker room to take a piss and then I went out the door but instead of going back to the field I went the other way around the side of the building to the back of the school just to see what was there and blow off some steam. There was nothing much back there except bike racks and a field behind the school until I see all the way over by the side of the building 2 people and it's Renee and some guy. He doesn't go to Hutch Falls so he must go to RTS he's kind of short and thin and he has those "I'm an intellectual" glasses some people wear and a leather jacket which I have to admit is pretty cool and they're facing each other and they're right in each others faces really really really close and they're far enough away I can't hear what they're saying to each other but I can just tell they're fighting. Even though their faces are pretty close for fighting. And then this guy puts his hand on her shoulder and she whacks it off. And I wonder if I'm going to have to go over and beat the shit out of his scrawny ass and then he says something else and puts it back and this time she leaves it there.

I go back around the other side of the building the girls always seem to know guys from other schools and I don't see how they do it. How the fuck it just happens anyway I was maybe going to come around the other side and say hi just because I felt like I was spying on them or something and it would be better to let them know but then I realize they might be kissing and I didn't want to disturb them. I wonder about Renee seeing me hiding with some girl from another school somewhere and then I thought she might see me somewhere with Caroline but I didn't know if that would be good or if she'd look down on Caroline as a whacked-out black-clad druggie fuck-up or not.

And then I realize nobody knows. Because just a few weeks ago John McKnight said to Randy Brewer in the locker room these exact words - "She's gonna have to go out with somebody because what is she gonna do be a nun the rest of her life" and Randy Brewer said "You should make another move she was probably just in a bad mood the 1st 200 times she blew you off." John threw a dirty sock at Randy and the rest of us weren't really listening even though I bet everyone was but now even though before I didn't think she was necessarily going out with John or anybody else because wouldn't I of heard about it now I was sure and I was pretty psyched except now suddenly I realize who's this guy and is he her boyfriend. Except I'm not sure he is her boyfriend or anything serious. And they're not looking too happy. The next day after that I saw her about 50 times before Spanish when we're finally in Spanish I almost say "Hey I saw you at the RTS game" or "I saw you with that guy at RTS" and for once I'm praying for a dialogue drill with the verb IR which means go so I could say "Tu vas la game at RTS?" But I didn't know how to say "I saw you" which would be a problem. But sometimes because Mr. Eller says "Your primary objective is to be understood" you can act that stuff out like point to your eyes and just say "Tu". But I didn't say anything.

OK that story about Renee and the soccer game was the past and now I'm going back to the present which is still the past. I had a conflict with Mr. Rasfenjohn about this between the soccer game and the backrubs when referring to my last composition for Creative Composition and I think all the other 1s too he said my use of tenses has to improve. Specifically he said "You must keep a careful watch on your tenses because I am becoming confused too often." I said I'm just expressing myself. He paused then he said "but you could express your-self even more convincingly. It is disturbing your flow" and I said "I just like to write" and then he said "Yes yes alright". The thing is sometimes when you're writing about the past (which I usually am because I'm not standing there writing when something's happening I'm going home 1st and eating and a lot of times I'm busy with stuff and I write about some-thing that happened a couple weeks ago) I have observed that tenses are confusing because if you're writing in the future about the past then you use the past tense but what you're writing about is happening then (when you're writing about) so you use the present tense and pretty soon Mr. Rasfenjohn is like "it's disturbing your flow". And philosophically speaking is the past ever really past? No. It is always with us.

Anyway Caroline and Douglas switched. So she was doing his back. He was looking in front of him and his head was moving because of her rubbing him and her hands came over him in front of his shoulders as she really dug in there. I was wondering if me and Gillian and Kath were going to switch but we never did and then finally everyone just stopped. Me and Douglas went upstairs for drinks. I know Douglas a lot better now because over the last few weeks since a little before soccer ended we've hung out more mostly with the girls but a lot without them too in the parking lot after practice when there was practice and after school now that there's just school when we don't feel like going home a bunch of times and once he came over to just hang out. I know for example that his Dad is some kind of genius scientist who invents vacuum packing and things like that and his Mom's a scientist too and their idea of a good time is trigonometry. I know that Douglas gets As but doesn't like people to know because he thinks they're judgmental and I know that when he's weird around you at 1st it's because he doesn't know you and later when he trusts you he really trusts you. Like the Mafia. And he believes trust is the only real thing that matters. And I know that when Douglas gets mad he's dangerous and he can hurt somebody but I really just know this from him saying it I kind of doubt he would hurt anybody. He's a really nice person I think who hates the world and also most people. Whatever you're discussing he can show you the people are full of it for example if you say Mr. Zeldof is a boring teacher Douglas says he's part of a centuries old education conspiracy to bore us to death. I know what he means because Mr. Zeldof is so boring he puts himself to sleep and he's famous for sleeping if you're taking a quiz or a test and for snoring. I heard that 1 time he fell asleep when he was talking and crashed onto his desk but I don't know if that's true. Anyway though I don't think it's some conspiracy I don't take that stuff too seriously I just think Douglas is screwed up about it but once in a while even he laughs at how harsh he is and I respect that.

But here's the really big thing. Douglas doesn't get along with his parents and they don't get along with him. He thinks they're detached from the world and they think he's just a teenager who hasn't learned anything yet about the world so they let him do what he wants. Also they're always working so they don't even notice. So he can't stand to be home in the house with them. Even sleeping. So he never is he always crashes at somebodys house. The comments I heard before about Douglas not getting a good nights sleep at his house and about crashing at Gillians foreshadowed this problem. Basically Douglas doesn't live anywhere. I mean not really. But sort of.

Anyway the kitchen is dark and we didn't turn on a light but we could see especially when the fridge was open. We got ice and poured Cokes and Tabs and the house and everything was spooky quiet and I said "You've got Caroline all over you."

"That was just a backrub" he said.

"Yeah but still I wouldn't mind having her all over my back."

"She's not my type" Douglas said.

"What's your type?"

"I prefer someone stable. And smarter."

"She's got that boyfriend anyway" I said.

"That guy is a complete loser and not good enough for her" Douglas said.

I said "Yeah." We took some sips then Douglas said "If you thought you had a chance with a girl would you definitely make a move?"

"Sure."

"You would?"

"Yeah."

"You'd just lean over and do it?"

"Kiss them?"

"Yes."

I said "Yeah. It's just a kiss."

"It is not just a kiss it's the 1st move that decides if you get laid or not."

"Yeah" I said.

"You have to talk 1st to get the ball rolling. To get them in the mood."

"I don't know" I said.

"Then when you're talking it just happens."

"It's better not to talk. Women respond to men who just do it" I said.

"No women like to talk about it. Ask anyone."

"Not when you're about to get laid no way man they just want you to do it."

"Talking loosens them up. Girls are uptight about sex."

"Well you can't ask. You can't just say "Do you want it?" You sound like a Dork. You have to just make a move. With confidence."

Douglas said "I don't think so."

"Believe me."

"It's all about pleasing a woman" he said.

"Yeah" I said.

"I'll tell you something women like it hard. Like an animal. And fast when you really go for it. Like you're a fucking animal."

"VTS" I said. "Sometimes really slow though."

"True" said Douglas.

This was the 1st time me and Douglas really talked in depth about this stuff and I remember it. The girls were sitting there when we went back down they did 1 of those things where they got real quiet suddenly like they'd been talking about us or rubbing our backs. This was 1 of the Laws Of Physics that if you walk into a room and nobody's talking they were talking about you. Then Caroline said she wanted to walk to 7-11 which was about a mile away for of course cigs and Douglas and Kath said they'd go and I said I'd go but Gillian didn't feel like going and Kath said somebody should stay with her so I stayed. I went back to the couch and she was sitting on the floor with her arms behind her holding her up.

I like being alone with Gillian and in the basement. It wasn't a sex thing she had this new short haircut where you really saw more of her eyes and the way they blinked because there wasn't so much hair all around them and she blinked a lot and now that it was getting cold she wore pants but thin ones so you could still see how her legs were and I almost admit they were kind of sexy themselves but I didn't want them wrapped around me or anything I just liked being with her because she was easy to be with. But 1 thing I was wondering was if we were going to do more backrubs now that we were alone just the 2 of us and did I want to or not.

"So Richie's coming to meet her at 1:30" Gillian said. About Caroline.

"Is she sneaking out?" I said.

"I suppose. But I don't think her Mom cares" Gillian said.

"Really? Not at all?" I said.

"Not not at all. She just well she's a very permissive mother."

"Oh."

"So what do you believe in Jeremy?" she said.

"What?"

"What do you believe in?"

"What do you mean?"

"Well what do you care about what would you give your life for?"

"The constitution I guess" I said.

Gillian got mad for some reason at me and she said "You'd die for the constitution?"

"Maybe."

"Jeremy don't die for the constitution."

I didn't say anything.

"Jeremy promise me you won't die for the constitution."

"OK I won't die for the constitution. What would you die for?"

She thought for a minute and she put her head down so I couldn't see her then she looked up again and she said "For my family. For my children and my husband."

"I'd die for my wife" I said.

"That's the only thing I would die for" she said.

"Uh-huh" I said.

"Love" she said.

"Uh-huh" I said.

"I think that's how you know if your life is meaningful. Don't you? If you have things in your life that are so important you'd die for them like love."

"I just want to start having a meaningful Sophomore year" I said.

We laughed. Gillian is always good for talking about love and meaning and things like that with. Gillian I figure when she's 90 will still be talking and thinking about important things. Anyway we just sat there for a while. I guess a part of me was like does this chick dig me just because she's so intense and she was looking at me when she was talking about love and stuff in a very intense way. She's sort of that way with everybody. But I am a guy. I think Gillian needs somebody very serious and sensible not like Douglas who's serious but not sensible but more like somebody else we don't know. Anyway her Mom came home and she respected the privacy of the basement but then we went up and talked to her anyway until Caroline Douglas and Kath came back with Caroline holding her pack of cigarettes in her hand and not even caring that Gillians Mom saw them and Gillians Mom didn't say anything and talked to her like she wasn't holding any cigarettes. We went back down to the basement and Caroline stood at the basement door to the outside back yard smoking and blowing her smoke outside and Douglas and Gillian started to have some stupid argument about some war they both agreed the war was stupid but they were mad and arguing about who was right about why it was stupid. Then Kath got tired and we all decided to go. Kath called her Mom who said she'd drop us off and we put our jackets on and so did Gillian even though she wasn't going anywhere and we stood outside in the street talking and waiting for Kaths Mom and it was dark except for a few lights in peoples houses and lawns and it was pretty chilly so we were all moving around a little and there wasn't a single star or moon or anything in the sky and it was so quiet except for us kicking around and joking a little and watching Carolines smoke going up and waiting for Kaths Mom.

CHAPTER 10

CHRISTMAS VACATION IN GREAT BRITAIN

Where people in Hutch Falls go on Christmas vacation basically depends on how loaded you are very loaded people go skiing in places like Colorado or The Alps or to islands like The Bahamas where by the way they sometimes bring back big bags of pot which they basically give away there and they also smoke joints that are 2 feet long. I have more to say about this later regarding a story with me Caroline and some pot she got from her scum-bag boyfriend Richie. Anyway the less-loaded people sometimes go somewhere or just stay around and goof off and the not loaded at all people get Christmas jobs at The Mall which is always busy for the Christmas rush. As for how loaded I am I'd say medium but I'm not positive because my Dad doesn't talk about money except for saying not to spend it or saying how much he saved by buying the old broken refurbished piece of junk 1 of something that he claims is better anyway and we go on vacations but usually only to places like New Orleans or Santa Fe or San Francisco because that's what my Dad likes to do and would do even if he had all the rice in China. As for skiing my Dad thinks it's stupid and people who do it are stupid. 1 because you break your legs and 2 because it's a lot of money to spend just to break your legs. My Mom doesn't like to travel because she just doesn't but she always said "if we're going to go why don't we go to Europe or somewhere interesting" and finally my Dad said OK we're going to England. Then of course he went and read every book article and magazine ever written about England and he made a lot of phone calls and did research to find the cheapest hotels and he was happy when he found 1 $2 cheaper than the last 1 he found and he updated us every night at dinner about the prices and what he was learning about English history and cars and morals and everything else. Normally this was very boring and my Mom was in the kitchen for most of it but once in a while something started out boring but then suddenly got pretty good like his story about the Bentley factory in Crew England and the big strike there in the 1950s that led to rioting and unrest and ended up with every worker getting a free Bentley so these workers would come to work and then drive around London in these super expensive cars which surprised the hell out of the really rich people who had paid all that money for the same cars until the company ended up paying the workers almost double to get them to give the Bentleys back and not drive them around except there was 1 guy who would not give his up and drove up and down and up and down in front of the king and queens palace in his every weekend until the king finally noticed him and asked him to go away and he did.

Anyway we went to England for Christmas vacation. The 747 had an upstairs which was pretty cool. My favorite joke that I kept making was "I'm going upstairs." As for english people and England it's like The Land Of James Bond. Everything just feels different there because it's a foreign country. And that includes you. You're like "May I please have a scone madam" and "Why pray tell is my scone not being served immediately with my afternoon tea sir?" It's like you're someone else and like everyones weird but OK. Maybe babies see the world this way. The bathrooms are cold too.

My Dad of course found the cheapest hotel in Europe in 1 of his "Cheapest Weirdest and Grossest Places In The World" guidebooks but score 1 for Dad because this place was cool. It used to be the Iranian Embassy and then the Iranians or somebody I guess made it into a hotel but when it was the embassy it was very old style and fancy with big stairs and crystal chandeliers hanging over you and it was all still there. The only thing gone was the Iranians. Even my Mom liked it.

Anyway we go to all the museums where I'm bored and so's my Mom and so's Beth but Claire and my Dad are in Museum Heaven. Claire can look at a painting forever my Dad can look at the little plaque about who painted it and where and when and who gave it to the museum forever because it's like reading. Me and Mom and Beth finally have a revolt and declare we're not going with them to the National Museum Of Boring Paintings that day and we go off but then they go to go shop so I wander around England alone for a while and it's kind of cool and as I'm walking around and the Double Decker Buses are going by I was thinking some about Gillian and Caroline and Douglas and Kath. Looking back on the night with the backrubs I felt like we were all really getting to know each other. I mean they all knew each other before but I was glad I was getting to know them and really know them like who they really were and what they were like. Gillian was a really sensitive and sweet person who maybe wasn't as secure as she 1st seemed when you saw her standing there kind of the leader of the group and willing to talk to anybody and everything. She didn't tell me this but I think she's sad not totally but in a certain way like life is just sad sometimes. If you look at Gillian and how she's been effected by her parents divorce I don't really know. Douglas of course was sort of my main man now and even though he wasn't the "Hey Yo What's Up" type you could still tell he wanted to be friends he was a little wimpy and I thought sometimes just for no reason that maybe he resented me for being on the soccer team and wished he could be even though he acted like all that stuff was no big deal or even sucked. But maybe it's just hard to look a little funny or more nerdy and be serious and smart which everyone doesn't even know. Caroline was just Caroline. Lost in her screwed up world that I didn't understand but that was just where she was and Kath because her stomach hurt 49 out of every 50 minutes I still didn't know too much except for she had stomach problems. I felt bad I'd been mad about getting Gillian and Kath for the backrubs when Douglas got Caroline and giving backrubs to Gillian or Kath was good practice anyway so I'd be good at it when I needed to rub say Renees back and I thought about doing that and her saying "Ooooooh Jeremy!" Ever since I got to England I'd been missing Renee a lot like she was a whole country away. I'd forget about her for a while but then I'd remember her if we were on the underground or eating or in the hotel. I'd think about her and not always mentally but sometimes just picturing her face and thinking about her without really thinking anything.

Anyway there are 2 big hi-lights of the trip. 1 was when we went to the Changing Of The Guard at Buckingham Palace which is where the King and Queen live but I don't think they're ever really there. The Changing Of The Guard is a very fancy ceremony and you'd better not talk or burp or make any noise at all. 1st there are all these guards standing there in seriously the stupidest hats you ever saw the hats are made out of black fuzz and they're about 3 feet high. They're like Cat In The Hat hats. I don't know why anyone would ever wear something like that. These guys are supposed to be soldiers too but I'm sure if you wore a hat like that in a war the enemy would pretty much just laugh themselves to death. Maybe that's the point.

Anyway there's a big "DONGGGGG" and it starts. (By the way they do all this every 2 hours which when you hear what it is is amazing just because of what a big pain in the ass the whole thing is but the thing is they have to do it that often because all the tourists want to see it but also because 1 of the things about these guys is they're not allowed to move. At all. So you always see kids and sometimes grown-ups going up to them and making faces and seeing if they'll make a face back or something which they never do and supposedly they'll never move at all not even an inch so you can make faces or yell or swear or tickle the fuzz on their hat or even I suppose piss on them and they still won't move but if you did actually piss on them if it were me I personally would say Fuck The Rules and who needs this stupid job and go ahead and beat the crap out of you. Anyway because of standing so still which I think is harder than you think they have to change the guard every couple hours when the thing goes "DONG". Then around from behind the palace come all these horses with all new guards in red uniforms and giant hats on. The horses all line up in 3 big rows and the guards on them scream all kinds of commands you can't understand at all but obviously mean things like "Horse turn to the right" or "Horse turn to the left" and 1 where the horses don't do anything so either the horses all screwed up or it meant "Horses don't do anything." Then the guards who've been standing guard march over to the horses and their faces and heads are still still and only their legs are moving like robots or Nazis and then the other guys get off the horses and they get on and the other guys go to their posts and then everyone stands very still which is the most solemn part of the ceremony and that's when it happens. 1 of the horses starts to piss. Right in the front row and it's so quiet because of the ceremony going on you can hear the piss hitting the ground and it sounds like "Pssssschhh". And it goes on. And on. And on. At 1st I'm like "Uh-oh" but then I start giggling a little and I don't look but I can tell Beth and Claire next to me are laughing too and the piss's still going on and not losing any power at all. It won't be long before it's in the Guinness Book Of World Records for Longest Piss Ever. And I swear the guards are just standing there like nothing's even happening. And then I look at my Dad and he looks at me at the same second and raises his eyebrows like "these British people aren't as fancy as they think they are." Then we both laugh a little trying not to be loud. This is an example of

me and my Dad thinking the same thing is funny. An example
of us not thinking the same thing is funny which is usually is
Enderby. Enderby is the book with the krepitating I told you
about a long time ago. Even Mr. Rasfenjohn even though he's
heard of this book never read it it's the kind of book my Dad
reads. Not now but later I checked it out to see what he
thought was so funny and here it is:

PFFFRRRUMMMP.
    And a very happy New Year to you too Mr. Enderby! . . .
    Perrrrp.
    A posterior riposte from Mr. Enderby. . . .
    Querpkprrmp.
    You see? . . . But what has prettiness to do with greatness,
eh? . . . The extremities. The feet that trod Parnassus . . . Fish and
Heroes, his early poems. . . . Merciful heavens, the weakness of
the great . . . hand that photograph back to me this instant . . .
What, Charles, are they doing? The man and woman in the picture? They are minding their own business, that's what they're
doing.
    Bopperlop.
    Rest, rest, perturbed spirit. . . . Love, love, love. That's all that
some of you girls can think about . . .
    Porripipoop.
    The Horns Of Elfland.

OK so way to write a whole book about farting. Very nice. And
they don't even sound like farts. Farts sound more like pwwp-
wwpww or Pfscssgff or pwhpwhpwhpwh (like a helicopter).
Ha ha ha. Plus I'm like "grow up". If I'm too old for fart jokes

why isn't my Dad? It's because of his sense of humor which is very different from my sense of humor. Anyway it was 1 of the hi-lights of the trip.

The other 1 was later when we rented a car to drive outside of London to see a castle 1 where no one lived now. This castle was of course researched and put on the itinerary which my Dads secretary typed up before we left home. Beth was being an extra-pain in the ass lately and she didn't want to go basically if you took her anywhere other than the Beth Reskin Institute Of Make-Up And Sucking Up To More Popular Girls she was unhappy. I just think she's a very very typical teenager who has to rebel against everything. She's also so horny she's like British guys this and British guys that and they're so cute and "Oooh those accents" and sometimes she's not even talking to anybody when she says it or at least nobody's listening. Anyway my Dad said she had to go and couldn't stay alone in London shopping so she was pissed all day my Mom though didn't mind going even though normally castles aren't her thing because they had big gardens there.

So we drive about 2 hours to get to this castle. It's pretty much just like you'd picture a castle big and stone and surrounded by forests and gardens. It's funny how castles can be pretty cool and totally boring at the same time it's cool because it looks really cool like a fairy tale and it's old and you can picture where the kings and queens walked around and where they shot arrows and where they dumped the boiling hot oil on the heads of their enemies from (how much would that suck?). But it's boring just because it is. There's nothing to really do there you just walk around and maybe pretend you're the King and Renee is the Queen and you get what-

ever you want and she thinks you're the greatest and sometimes even calls you sire like "Sire perhaps you'd like to have
some more sex now." And when you get pissed off you can
behead people even though your Mom's like "You shouldn't
behead so many people." When we were walking around I
imagined Renee about to be beheaded by rebellious peasants
pissed off by the castle and how rich everybody there was and
everything when all they had was manure and rice and hard
work. I was on their side in terms of fairness but I couldn't let
Renee who was a Princess die when I loved her so much so I
rode my valiant steed in and at the last second when the guil-
lotine started falling I jumped under it with my horse and
grabbed the rope it hangs from and pulled it out of the big
contraption. Then before anybody could do anything I got off
grabbed Renee and her head out of the bottom part and
pulled her with me onto my horse and took off. They could
still burn the castle and they did.

At night we head back to London my Mom is driving and
the roads there aren't all lit up the way they are in America.
And it's really dark. We're on lots of side roads and stuff because that's how you get around in England and basically we
get lost my Dad has about 50 maps but you know what? Maps
don't do you much good when you don't know where you are
in the 1st place.

Now being lost is bad enough but we're all starving to
death too because there was no food at the castle and all we
ate was bread and cheese and apples my Dad bought at the
lame British grocery store. This is what we eat every day by
the way for lunch because my Dad says "Why waste valuable
time sitting down to eat when you're on vacation and you have

things to do and you can eat a perfectly delicious lunch of bread and cheese and fruit" which isn't not true. Especially when you put the cheese on the apple which my Dad invented. It is good but not every day. And not that good. And what my Dad really means is "Why waste money on some real lunch when I don't want to?" So it's late and we're hungry and lost and London and our hotel are nowhere to be found a few times we go through little towns or villages but there's no one around to ask for directions. My Dad keeps looking at the map and saying "if we're here then we should do this but if we're there then we should do that" and my Mom's not listening to him and then we drive into 1 of the little towns and we go right through it without seeing a single person and then we're on sort of the outskirts of the town and my Mom makes a turn and suddenly we're going down. Not fast but definitely down and it's bumpy we all look out the windows and there's only a few stars out so you can't see anything but then Claire by the other window from me says "there's a rail." And I squint because it's dark out the window and there's a rail right next to the car. I mean right next to it. "We're on a staircase" I say.

"Why would there be a staircase here?" my Mom says and she keeps going.

She's got a point and we still can't really see anything but there is the rail and the whole going down evidence.

"Honey it's a staircase" my Dad says.

"No it isn't."

"You should stop" my Dad says.

"I'm not stopping I want to get back to the hotel" my Mom says. "Everyone shut up."

"Annie you're driving down a staircase" my Dad says.

Finally my Mom stops and then she growls like a dog which I never heard her do before. She waited a second then we tried to go back up the staircase but the car won't go back up. Finally we got out and we were 1/2 way down a long staircase that went down to some little park.

My Dad took over the drivers seat and tried to back the car back up the stairs but it still won't go. We discussed forward but it was a bad idea too because there was no way out of the park down there finally my Dad said "I'm going to go for help."

"I want to go back to the hotel" my Mom said.

"Well honey the car's stuck" my Dad says.

"I know the car's stuck" my Mom says.

"Then how come you're not acting like it" my Dad says.

"I am acting like it" my Mom says. "This is how I act."

"Well it's not very helpful" my Dad says.

"Oh is that right?" my Mom says.

Anyway we decided we would all go and we left the car there 1/2 way down the stairs and walked back to the town together as hungry and pissed off as we all were there was something cool about being on that dark road in the middle of nowhere at night by ourselves walking in Europe. I thought. I drew a connection between that night and the beautiful dark night in Wyoming last summer when I looked up at the stars. Anyway we got to town and we knocked on some guys door (really knocked because they don't have doorbells in England) and he called a tow truck which took about 2 hours to get there so my Dad asked him for directions to a Pub and it turns out that's where all the people were and we ate fish and chips which my Dad liked because it was fish and I liked because it was good and then the truck dragged the car back up the stairs and the driver thought it was pretty funny and so did all the people in the Pub who I told about it but my Mom didn't think it was funny until I was telling about the 10th group of people who wanted to hear the story and then finally she smiled a little and put her face in her hands and said "Oh Abe" and then she just cracked up. We got directions and drove back to London.

PREFACE

"You can't just follow the herd." My Dad believes that and I think he's right. Because if there's a bunch of cows or horses or anything and you're a cow or a horse and you just follow them you never know where they might go. Off a cliff? Into a valley or some quicksand? Through a minefield? So the theme of this chapter is will I or won't I follow the herd.

CHAPTER 11

WILL I OR WON'T I FOLLOW THE HERD?

Caroline didn't go anywhere on Christmas vacation but she didn't work in The Mall either if Caroline was going to get a job she'd work in a dungeon in the city or something like that. She just hung out the whole time. The 1st day back I ran into her in the hall we were being kind of smushed by everyone going by and I was so close to her face I saw under her make-up like when you look at someone really close and you can see their pores. And I could smell her perfume which I didn't really know before that second she wore because I guess you had to be really close to smell it. She was holding her red back-pack in her hand and I said "Hey" and then I told her about England and the stairs but not about the horse pissing. She said "Richie went on a trip to The Bahamas he was going to take me but the ticket fell through. But guess what?"

"What?" I said.

"Guess what he brought me?"

"I don't know. Something from The Bahamas?"

"A quarter ounce of Ganga. From The Bahamas."

"Wow."

"They grow like the very best in the world there."

"Wow."

"We're going to smoke it Friday night."

"OK" I said.

That night I called Caroline. I never called her before mostly I talked to Gillian and Kath I talked to about 3 or 4 times when she called me and just talked and Douglas and me weren't talk to each other on the phone guys but Caroline was more off with her idiot boyfriend a lot and besides she was too busy smoking to have a conversation for more than 30 seconds before she had to go outside for another cigarette anyway but it had been really good seeing her in the hall and reconnecting after Christmas vacation and I decided to call her.

Her Mom answered the phone and then she got her.

"Hello?"

"Hey it's Jeremy."

"Oh. Hi Jeremy."

Usually here Gillian or whoever says something but Caroline didn't.

"So we're meeting Friday?" I said.

"Uh-huh" she said.

Then she said "So what's new?"

"Not much" I said. "How about you?"

"Nothing."

"Oh" I said. Then I said "How's Richie?"

"He's great he's putting together this big deal for distribution rights right now."

"For what?" I said.

"I'm not sure."

"Oh."

"He's real busy."

"Wow" I said.

Then I waited another second then I said "Well I'll see you tomorrow."

"OK bye."

"Bye."

Anyway I wish I hadn't called her and I pictured her calling Gillian and saying "Guess what Jeremy just called me" but Gillian would defend me and say she talked to me on the phone all the time and I was totally capable of having a good conversation. But if she called Kath Kath would say "You know he's got a crush on you don't you" because Kath thinks everyone has a crush on everyone and I don't but try convincing any hot girl you don't have a crush on her. Not that Caroline is exactly hot. But this all got superseded anyway that Friday night when we met at Carolines. Don't think I didn't discuss this with Douglas 1st at school when I said "these girls don't get that Pot's bad for you" I said.

"Pot's not bad for you" he said.

"It kills your brain cells and gives you lung cancer."

Douglas didn't like cigarettes so I was assuming he didn't smoke Pot but then he goes "Pot's all natural. It's from Mother Earth."

I was like Mother Earth??

"So you've smoked Pot?" I said.

"Yes."

"A lot?"

"I wouldn't necessarily say I've smoked a lot" he said.

"Huh" I said.

"It's quite wonderful" he said. "Have you ever felt like your brain was floating?"

"Not really" I said.

I didn't even really want to go to Carolines because everyone but me would be smoking Pot but I didn't want to be such an idiot I didn't even show up so I went. Caroline lives in an apartment complex called Blue Court where the buildings are blue. Her and her Mom and her sister live on the 1st floor of 1 of the buildings. The whole place smelled like it was made out of plastic or something especially in the halls and inside. In their apartment there was the living room where you watched TV and ate and hung out and her and her sister shared a bedroom with all these stuffed animals that I figured were her sisters but then when she was showing me the bedroom she introduced them - "this is Eleanor" who was a rabbit and "that's Pudge" who was a falling apart dirty and definitely a senior citizen type stuffed animal who I couldn't tell exactly what animal he once was and she laughed like "I know this is pretty queer" but you could tell she loved them and most of them were hers and not her little sisters. Then her Mom had a bedroom where the bed wasn't made and there were shoes on the floor which would make my Mom raise her eyebrows and go "Hmmmmm" and there was 1 very little bathroom in-between the bedrooms but Caroline was obviously used to it and when you're used to something it doesn't bother you.

Anyway 1st her Mom was there and instead of being like a grown-up Caroline she was kind of fat and wore no black at all she looked like someone you kind of think has 32 kids and a husband drinking beer. She seemed nice but mostly she was in the kitchen sitting down at the table reading a magazine until she went out to dinner with her girlfriends.

As soon as she left we went into Carolines room and we turned on her stereo and sat on the floor and Caroline got some beers from under the bed and passed them out (she didn't say but I'm sure Richie got them for her). I took some sips because I'm allowed to have basically as much of my Dads beer at dinner as I want anyway but it was warm and gross I wondered why she didn't put them in the freezer for a couple minutes but everyone else was drinking them and not complaining.

So of course Caroline puts on Pink Floyd The Wall which is kind of depressing not so much the words which I'm not listening to and which are all about rebellious kids and rebelliousness and school sucking in every song but more just the music which I basically hate but which has some good parts. And then she goes into her closet and comes out and says "OK let's go".

I didn't know we were going anywhere but we got up and everyone put on their jackets and we left and started walking to Nierbeck Woods instead of going in the main entrance we turned up the hill and went in there but everyone I guess knew where we were going because after going through the woods a little we got to this big rock I'd never seen before where obviously they were going and nobody else was around anywhere because it wasn't on any of the trails. It was pretty dark but not too dark to see. The rock had a big flat part and Gillian and Douglas sat there and Caroline and Kath sat on the ground and I leaned against it Caroline got a big baggie of Pot out of her pocket and rolling papers and matches. Her and Douglas each got a rolling paper and put some Pot on it and rolled it up and basically licked it all over and closed it which I can't believe no one is grossed out by not that I'm some kind of Howard Hughes live in a mansion by myself freak but at least if I were going to smoke Pot I'd want to smoke 1 I licked myself or Caroline licked and not Douglas. So Caroline lights a match and lights hers and takes a really long drag and then she leans back and really sucks it in and then she laughs and then she starts coughing like her throats going to come out her mouth and land on the ground but no matter how hard she's coughing she's laughing inbetween each cough and the effect of all this I think is there isn't a whole lot of oxygen going into her head and she turns as red as you can turn and still be alive. Like a tomato. Gillian and Douglas by the way sit on the ground now against the rock and I sit down where I am and lean against the rock too. Meanwhile Gillian takes a puff and she smiles while she holds it inside which is what you do with Pot to get really high and then Kath goes and then she passes it to me.

"No thanks" I say.

Kath is still holding her puff in but finally she says "Well just pass it to Douglas" and I reach up and I take it and now I'm holding Pot.

I pass it to Douglas and then next time when it comes around I'm like a pro at Pot passing and it goes around about 3 times and when it's almost gone they keep smoking it even though they're practically smoking their fingers now and I have to pass it 1 time when basically I'm just passing burning fire and I think I didn't yell "Ouch" and then finally it was gone beyond a shadow of a doubt or at least I thought it was but no it turns out Douglas finds the last little bit of Pot in there at the bottom and taps it with his finger into a new joint he's rolling. You don't waste any Pot.

The next joint goes around and by now it smells like Pot everywhere and Douglas is giggling now even though he's the only person I know who can giggle and still look depressed. Gillian is like "Oh wow everything's amazing I love you guys" and she's looking up at the sky where you mostly see trees and some sky and stars inbetween the branches. Caroline meanwhile has an attitude like "I'm way more a Pot pro than you guys AND you're kind of stupid but that's OK for rookies like you."

Then Gillian's like "Let's take a walk" and Kath who's in her own world where maybe she's plotting to secretly murder someone is like "OK" and Douglas gets up to go but Caroline says "I'm too mellow" and I say "Me too" and they go without us. Me and Caroline don't say anything for a while then she lies down on the ground and starts to hum something I think Pink Floyd this goes on for a while then I lie down too but because of where I'm sitting when we lie down we're not that next to each other the ground which is grass and dirt is sort of soft and hard and it's mellow looking up at the trees and the sky. Caroline stops humming and then I hum a little bit of All Out Of Love but I feel kind of stupid so I hum part of the song so it's different than it really goes then I stop and Caroline goes "What's that?"

"I don't know" I say.

"It's nice" she says.

"Yeah" I say.

"Here put your head here" she says touching her head and I kind of spin around and move up so the tops of our heads are right next to each other but our feet are in opposite directions so we're like 1 long line. Suddenly I can smell her wearing the same perfume I smelled her wearing in the hall at school inside the Pot smell which is drifting away.

"You get more vibes when your heads are close" she says.

"Vibes are cool" I say.

"They come from your whole body" Caroline says.

"Oh" I say.

"They're very soothing. You know it's like calm."

She's quiet for a long time it seems like she's thinking about something and then she says "You never got hi?"

"No" I say.

"The 1st time I got hi I was like this is the greatest thing in the world."

"Really?" I said.

"It's the fruit of the Earth Jeremy."

Here we go again but I didn't really think that then.

"What's so great about it?" I say.

"It's like - it's like" and she waits a second then she says "my mind is turned off."

"It goes off?"

"I'm a very different person. Still me but not me do you know what I mean?"

"Are you somebody else?"

She laughed a little in this short way.

"I can't explain it. You'll experience it some day."

I didn't know how she knew this but she seemed sure in her own crazy Caroline Zisko where you know things you don't know and don't know things you should way.

Then she said "I was with a guy over the summer when he smoked Pot for the 1st time. He just giggled for about 3 hours everybody was like shut up. But we all thought it was funny too. It's annoying."

A minute later I said "what happened to you over the summer?"

"What?"

"You said before, a long time ago it was really bad and you didn't want to talk about it."

She didn't say anything and I thought she was asleep or didn't hear me because she was hi. Or she just didn't want to say anything. But then 2 or 3 minutes later she goes "Oh I just stopped eating and got sick and tried to kill myself and fooled around with every guy in Glades Florida."

I was like 'Uh-oh'. I figured if she tried to kill herself she could try again and I wanted to say the right thing so she wouldn't, and I said "Wow."

"I hadn't seen my Dad in 3 years just about and I had this super-smart idea I'd spend the summer with him. In Florida. You know my Mom she's nuts but she's not crazy you can have a conversation with her she has some idea what's going on in like hello reality but my Dad is like you can't even say anything to him he just moves around like some old guy and doesn't say anything. He didn't leave my Mom for another woman you know or anything like that he lives by himself in this apartment. He likes the weather there. And he doesn't mind if I'm there he's just in the kitchen filling up his stupid thermos all the time anyway. But it's like I don't know Night Of The Living Freaking Dead there it drives you nuts. Anyway I meet this guy at the shirt shop I'm working at and he turns out to be a jerk. So are his friends and I've lost 20 pounds in the 1st 2 weeks I'm there. At work they're like "Caroline". But I swear just the idea of food makes me sick. I almost got a job as a hostess. Thank God I didn't get that job."

She stopped talking and took a really deep breath that was like "Oh man". Then she said "So I took 26 aspirin. They pumped my stomach. I did something to my intestines. Don't take aspirin if you ever want to kill yourself."

I figured I was supposed to be giving her advice on not killing herself versus her giving me advice on how to kill myself and I said "You should never want to die."

Caroline puffed up her cheeks with a mouth full of air and then a second later said "I know."

"What did your Dad say?"

"He brought me flowers. Red roses. At the hospital like I was getting married. Then at the hospital they're like Your father's so nice and You have to start eating and You have to go into counseling and change your life. I did start eating. I don't know why I guess I was hungry."

After a long time nobody came back and although we thought it was possible they'd been killed or eaten by a bear or a lunatic psycho killer we figured they were just lost and it was getting cold so we went back. We laid down again in Carolines room with our heads next to each other but not as close finally I heard everybody coming in the door and I sat up pretty fast. "It's soooooooo beautiful out" Kath said. She was sort of leaning on Douglas the truth is Kath looked happier than I ever saw her before in her life which almost makes me think Pot not only isn't bad but maybe people should smoke it all the time. Gillian says "Where were you guys" and I said "We came back" and she said "We were worried about you" and I said "It got cold." Douglas wasn't really listening he came up to me and said "How are you man?" and I said "Fine" but I said it slow like I was hi like "Fiiiine" which was moronic but they were probably way too hi to notice anyway. Then Gillian said "You should try new things. Loosen up Jeremy stop being such a stick in the mud." I felt like saying "Sorry I don't want to kill all my brain cells and probably get arrested some day" but I didn't and I could tell by her face Gillian felt bad and then she said "To each his own". "Or her" Caroline said and she's been totally quiet since they came back so it was like the dead person on the floor suddenly saying something and we were all like "Oh - Caroline's here."

"That's not the expression" Gillian said.

"So what" Caroline said.

"It's not the expression it's to each his own" Gillian said.

"You're the big feminist" Caroline said.

"This is very negative" Douglas said.

They shut up.

We lay around at Carolines until really late. I called home and told my Mom I'd be late I had to call if I was coming home after 12:00 on a weekend. Douglas drove us all home because he had his license now. Carolines mother never came home and they smoked again in the back behind the building and we all got super mellow. Caroline played Yellow Submarine by the Beatles and it was kind of like "Whoa we're in the 60s" but mostly just nobody was mad or unhappy and it was like time or something was moving kind of slowly all over us and I felt like sometimes you find people just like you and these guys were.

CHAPTER 12

DOUGLAS HERO FOR A DAY

There's this guy Christopher Lemon in our class who's Mr. Student Union and Mr. Plan Homecoming and Mr. Do Everything and everyone lets him do everything because who cares and somebody's got to do it. He wears a tie to school for no reason and he's friends with this group of guys who sit around and think a lot. Anyway Christopher's up giving this speech during MooSoo (Mandatory Student Union) about apathy and how it's rotting the student body from within and how it's a cancer we have to cure and we have to all care more about everything. When he's done talking he asks if there are any questions and a few people make comments about how apathy is bad I'm sitting next to Gillian all the way on 1 side in the middle and I whisper to her "People care he's just pissed because they don't care about the same things he cares about like keeping the halls clean. And class spirit."

Gillian whispers back "That's a really good comment you should say that."

"Now?" I say.

"It's a really good comment."

I'm like I don't think so. Then Gillian says "well if you're not going to say it tell Douglas to say it."

So I tell Douglas the comment and then I say "Gillian thinks you should say it."

And Douglas raises his hand and Christopher calls on him a second later and he gets up and says "In my opinion you think there's so much apathy because everyone doesn't care about precisely the same issues you care about. For example school spirit. And how clean the Lunchroom is hygienically speaking. But people do care they just care about different issues. For example how cool they are and who's dating who and what they're wearing."

Douglas sits down and people start cheering. Christopher starts trying to argue. Finally we end up making a resolution which passes that apathy is a cancer and the student body of Hutch Falls High School will have less apathy.

The whole rest of the day people are coming up to Douglas and saying "Great Comment" and some girls are smiling at him and you'd think he just read the declaration of independence or something. Plus what he said was kind of weird because he was saying it was fine to just care about your clothes which was not exactly my point but nobody really paid attention to that they were more just like "that was cool". People can be narrowminded like that.

Anyway I'll tell you now what's so amazing about Gillian she just really understands people. I walked her home after school which I do a lot because we live mostly in the same direction and it was cold and I had on my big blue down coat I just got because I got too tall for the red down coat I had in 8th Grade and Freshman Year I knew that coat looked stupid like the Michelin Man but it fit so I figured I should still wear it until finally I could go to my Dad and show him it really didn't fit anymore. Beth of course gets new coats every year and my Dad harumphs a little about it but doesn't say anything because girls have to worry more about fashion and how they look. Anyway Gillian who wore many types of clothes had on a red scarf wrapped around her mouth and a hat (I think it was black) with a white pom on top. It was cold but I don't wear hats. There was some snow on the ground from a few nights before when it snowed all night and I made a snowball to throw at nobody in particular and Gillian said "So do you wish you made that comment?"

"No. Douglas made it" I said.

"But he got all the credit" Gillian said. "For your comment."

"That's OK" I said.

"I guess" she said. Then she said "I could never make a comment in front of everyone."

"Why not?" I said.

"Oh I don't know I'm too insecure."

"No you're not."

"I am."

"I don't mind talking in front of people but I don't like to get up and make a big deal out of every little thing" I said.

"Oh" said Gillian.

"There's better things to do with your time" I said.

"I suppose."

We walked a little bit and over Gillians scarf I could tell her eyes looked sad or something and I said "what's new?"

She said "Nothing. With you?"

"Nothing" I said.

"I suppose it would be nice well to be less shy" she said.

"Being shy isn't the end of the world" I said.

"I'd just like to be oh I don't know more confident."

I couldn't believe Gillian didn't think she was confident because even though I noticed before she was more insecure than I realized I thought she was very confident even more than me. She was almost like the leader of our little group.

"You're confident" I said. "You're very confident."

"Do you think so?"

"Yeah" I said.

"Well I didn't like Douglas getting all the credit for your comment" she said.

"Oh" I said.

"And it was my dumb idea."

"But I wouldn't say it so it's better he said it than nobody saying it."

"I suppose" Gillian said.

When we got to her house she said "Do you want to come in for some coffee?"

I said "Yeah. It's freezing."

We sat in her kitchen and she made coffee in the coffee pot. It was really strong. Gillian was sitting there at the kitchen table which was round and wood and had salt shakers and stuff in the middle you could see out into her back yard through the window in the back door and also see the tops of trees there through the windows over the sink. She said "I'm just the kind of person who believes life's a journey you know? And you can let your journey go past you or you can go on your journey. And it's a waste of what Gods given you if you don't go."

"God?" I said.

"Well whoever."

"And who knows what your journey is? I mean does my Dad know if my journey includes college? No. That's the journey he wants me to take" I said.

"I suppose. But you should go to college."

"Why?"

"Because it opens up the world. It gives you more opportunities more journeys you can take from there."

"I guess" I said.

The truth is I was bummed out a little even though Gillian was definitely my closest friend and we were drinking coffee and hanging out and everything was great I don't really know why not because of Douglas and the comment. Maybe more just because things were going along and sometimes things just going along is kind of a bummer. Maybe I learned that from Gillian but maybe I learned it somewhere else in the story.

CHAPTER 13

OUR DAY IN THE CITY

Stuff happens and you learn to live with it. We all have a lot in life. A fate. A destiny.

For example I am Jeremy Reskin and I live in Hutch Falls New Jersey and this was my fate. I have 2 sisters Claire and Beth 1's a pain in the ass 1 isn't. My Mother loves me and worries about me and isn't as crazy as most other mothers. Her and my Dad are still married because it's the destiny of other people like Gillian and Caroline that their parents are divorced. My Dad makes pretty good money. He likes being a father. He commutes to work in New York. And he loves more than just about anything Mo Levitsky.

Mo Levitsky is the guy who owns Mo Levitskys. Mo Levitskys is where my Dad buys his clothes. And sometimes my clothes. It's down all these weird little streets on the 3rd floor of this building that looks like nobody's been in it in 50 years in the Garment District in New York. Which if they asked me before they named it I would of told them we don't really call them garments anymore. But whatever. Anyway once a year there's a day when I skip school and spend the day in New York with my Dad it's called Our Day In The City and maybe other kids on a day like that would go to a baseball game or go for a bike ride with their Dads but we go to Mo Levitskys.

The thing is this year I'm not psyched to go not that I was ever that psyched but it was OK and it beat school but now I want to see Renee in Spanish and the only day my Dad can go the week he wants to go is a Wednesday when we have Spanish not to mention I want to hang with Gillian and everybody on the balcony so at dinner when my Dad says "Jeremy how about Our Day In The City this Wednesday" I say "that's not really a good day."

"Do you have a test?" my Dad says.

Like having a test would make me not want to miss school.

"No" I say.

"Then let's go."

My Mom is looking at me with her "The world's caving in" look and I say "I'm not really supposed to miss school you know when you're a Sophomore and everything."

"But you like missing school" my Dad said.

"VTS."

"What?" my Dad said.

"Very True Statement."

"Don't you want to have Our Day In The City?" he said.

So I said "Yeah but what about Thursday" when there was at least no Spanish.

"I can only get free on Wednesday and it's Mo Levitskys

Overstock Sale this week you want to go to the Overstock Sale don't you?"

The night before we were going when I went to bed here's what I thought about that Russia was going to invade America tomorrow and they'd break into Hutch Falls High and go to Spanish and because Renee was the hottest girl there they'd say "Come veeth us!!!" and no one would ever hear from her again. Meanwhile me and my Dad would be in Mo Levitskys which the Russians probably couldn't even find. But I'd say I had to go help Renee and my Dad would try to talk me out of it but I'd go to the Russian HQ and I'd see through the fence the building they were taking her to and I'd dig under the fence and elude the sentries and climb into a window and she'd be tied to a chair with her shirt off but her bra on and there'd be all these soldiers around and from the looks in their eyes even though they were speaking Russian we'd all know they were going to rape her and she'd know too and she'd look over and see me at the window and I'd give her a signal not to look because they'd see me and she'd look away and I'd realize I needed a plan because there were about 10 or 20 of them and I couldn't beat up that many. So what I did was I went in another window to the room next door and I started a fire in the garbage can and then I yelled really loud in this weird voice so they wouldn't know I was yelling in English like "Yooowwweennaaasaaaaaaaaahh!!!" and then I went back out the window and back in the other window and most of the soldiers had gone to see what the noise was all about but there were 3 of them left and 1 of them was ripping off Renees bra and her Tits flew out and then he ripped her panties off with

1 hand and there she was with her pubic hair, just sitting there and you could see a little under it and she went "Oh!" and I could see she was shaking from being so scared and just as he was about to grab 1 of her Tits with his dirty Russian hand I said "excuse me" and he turned around and I grabbed him in a wrist lock and threw him into the other 2 soldiers who were coming at me and they all toppled to the ground and Renee went "Oh. Jeremy" and I untied her but then the other soldiers were coming back and I stood next to the door and kept elbowing them in the face when they came in but finally 1 of them got by and pointed his gun at me and I knew it was curtains for me when Renee went "Hey" and the soldier turned around to look at her and she smiled and took 1 Tit in her hand and kind of squeezed it a little and pointed it at him and his mouth opened and his face just about fell off his head and then I kicked him in the balls and grabbed Renees hand and I said "thanks". And she said "It was my turn". And I lifted her up and out through the window and when I climbed up after her I looked around for her clothes and I found her panties and she put them back on but I couldn't find her bra so her Tits were going to have to stay naked and we ran into the woods and when we were pretty far away we stopped and Renee put her hands around me and she said "what are we going to do? The Russians have taken over". And I said "I'll take care of the Russians". And she smiled and turned around and then she leaned forward against a tree and said "I think you need a little reward".

Anyway I slept late and my Dad went downtown to get some work done. Then I went to the train station it was raining a little bit and I got that weird feeling you get when you're supposed to be in school and you're not and everyone else is. Like you're the only person left on the planet. And you're going to get in trouble for not being there. In New York though there are lots of kids out because there always are I don't know if it's because a lot of kids in New York don't go to school or if everyone in New York just gets to sign out for lunch or they're tourists or what. I go to my Dads building which is this black building with black windows and a really fancy lobby with marble floors like The Acropolis in Ancient Greece and I go up to his office which is on the 35th floor. I breeze right past the secretary at the front and I stop at the door of my Dads office until he looks up and says come in. His office is pretty medium-size and really messy with papers and folders and law books all over the place. He's not ready yet and he goes into his drawer to get out this set of blocks that he's been giving me to play with since I was about 3. They're in a little yellow box there's about 6 of them 1 square, 1 round, 1 square with like an arrow shaped chunk cut out of it, 1 like a tube, and I can't remember the other ones. They're all different colors pretty faded after all these years yellow and red and green wood. Here's what they look like.

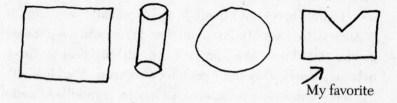

My favorite

And I can't believe my Dad is still giving them to me like someone 15 years old wants to play with blocks! This is a problem with my Dad not getting it about my being more of an adult anyway he takes out the blocks and he says "Here the blocks."

"I'm a little old for blocks Dad."

So I go and sit on the couch and just wait for him. I have to admit though I was so bored I did kind of want to play with them.

Anyway when my Dad is finally ready to go he takes 1 of those plastic hair brushes he uses that basically brush your hair by ripping it out of your skull out of his drawer and brushes his hair. Then he hands it to me and I use it even though this is basically like child abuse. Once most of my hair is on the brush instead of on my head we go.

The 1st stop of course is Tannebaums Deli. Tannebaums Deli is small and really crowded and it's the best corned beef on Earth and at 1/3 the price of the pricier delis everybody else goes to. My Dad calls it a premier deli. It's a pretty big deal to go to Tannebaums Deli but it's really near my Dads office and I wonder if he goes there all the time like every day or 2 who would stop him? In general he has this whole life in the city and nobody knows anything about it except Tannebaums and Mo Levitskys and he works. Maybe he has another secret family here! But I doubt it. He's not that type.

Anyway they say "Hello Counselor" to him when we come in like they know him and he's a pretty big deal at Tannebaums maybe they don't get a lot of lawyers. We blow off the menu because we know we're having corned beef and chocolate egg creams and when it comes the sandwiches are so big the bread on top is basically hanging on to the sandwich for dear life. There's also big pieces of corned beef and huge pieces of fat hanging down over the sides my Dad puts on lots of hot mustard and so do I even though I like the yellow mustard better because my Dad frowns on the yellow mustard and thinks it's for kind of low-life people who don't appreciate good food and flavor.

Anyway we take our 1st huge bites which you can barely get in your mouth and we're chowing down when my Dad says "So Jeremy lets talk about your grades."

Here's some background history: We had a discussion over the summer where my Dad pretty much decided my grades were going to improve and 1st Semester it didn't exactly happen that way. I already got nailed for that when we got back from England when 1st Semester grades came and my Dad calmly freaked out and explained the concept of responsibility and consequences to me which apparently I didn't understand. But now Mr. Crain (my academic counselor) called my Dad at his office to tell him he spoke to my teachers and I wasn't doing any better yet this semester and I never came to see him to receive any counseling about classes and homework. Mr. Crain stopped me in the hall and told me he called so I was waiting for this talk and here it was.

"Your Mother and I both felt we had an agreement with you that you would improve your grades."

"I'm doing the best I can" I said.

"I don't believe that."

"Well believe it" I said. I paused for a second because that was a little harsh. He kind of squinted a little.

"Jeremy I know you're young and the future seems like it's

a long way away. But you will be applying to college in under 2 years and your grades are going to determine where you get in."

"College isn't for everybody" I said.

Not many things make my Dad stop eating his corned beef at Tannebaums but this was 1 of them.

"Maybe not but it's for everyone in this family" he said with his mouth stuffed with his corned beef.

"I'm not doing that bad" I said. "Probably mostly Bs. And a couple Cs. Maybe 1 D+ or C−. A lot of kids get mostly Ds."

"We're not talking about a lot of kids we're talking about you. Is that the highest standard you want to set for yourself?"

I hated when he asked questions like that it didn't seem like you could answer them except the way he wanted you to. For once I wanted to say "why yes that's the highest standard I want to set for myself" but instead I said "not really".

"Alright then. Lets work from there what would you like to achieve?"

"More Bs I guess."

"That would be a start."

"Maybe another A (I already got 1 1st Semester in Creative Comp)."

"Alright then."

"I could probably do better in English. Math I just suck at though and I've got Trig this semester which is even worse than geometry. And I've got Mr. Scow for American History. He's a really weird guy. A total freak. Everybody who had him 1st Semester said your grades aren't related to what you do in his class."

"Then start with English. What are the problems you're having?" my Dad said.

"The papers I guess. They're stupid I mean we just read The Grapes Of Wrath by John Steinbeck. I read it. Most of it but then Mr. Fasbek wants us to write a paper about it and I don't know what to write about there's nothing to write."

"Of course there is" my Dad says.

"Like what?"

"Well you could write about about" my Dad says repeating about twice and then he looks up at the sky waving his hand with his corned beef in it around like there are about a million things you could write about and he says "about how 2 of the characters - how 2 of the characters - the interaction between 2 of the characters."

"Like what?"

"Like what they say to each other. And how they act."

"Yeah but I don't know how do you write a paper about that?"

"You just write it" my Dad said.

"Oh" I said.

"Now what about history? Your teacher can't be that bad."

"Oh yeah? When was the last time you went to school?"

Because I was going along with my Dads plan to make a plan I could get away with saying stuff like that to him then.

"What is it exactly about this teacher?" my Dad said.

"Scow just wants you to copy dates and stuff from the book into the papers but then he's like what's your interpretation? I don't know I don't have an interpretation."

"You should have an interpretation."

"Why? I mean if I know all the stuff."

"Because that's how you learn and because you have to interpret in college and after college in life."

"I'm not really into interpretation."

"Tough luck."

We didn't say anything for a second.

"What did you write your last paper on?" my Dad said.

"The Industrial Revolution."

"Okay. What about it were you studying?"

"How bad it was for the workers who actually did all the work."

"Fine there's your interpretation the Industrial Revolution was very painful for the people - the people who - who did it."

I said "Yeah but it did a lot of good things too. All sorts of stuff got built and a lot got accomplished."

"Right. Good there's the interpretation a lot of people got hurt but a lot got accomplished. That's your interpretation."

"I just said that."

"I know. And there it is an interpretation."

"Dad that's not an interpretation it's just what Mr. Scow said 20 million times in class."

"It's still an interpretation. And it's a good start I think you know more than you give yourself credit for." There was a pause and then he said "And to be Frank I'm also concerned you're not reading enough. It's very important for you to read more to cultivate reading as a habit a life long habit."

This was a lot like a rabbit telling you to cultivate carrot eating as a life long habit. My Dad said it to me about 40 million times since I was about 2.

Finally just when I was thinking we weren't going to talk about math Dad said "OK what about math?"

"I just can't do it" I said. "Can't I just not be good at something?"

"You can do anything you set your mind to" Dad said. "That grade has got to go up."

Thankfully that was the end of the talk and as sort of a celebration we ordered 2nd Egg Creams. My Dad then told me about some case he was working on for about an hour where some family business was breaking up and how the "Almighty Green" comes between families and how it's important not to let that happen.

When lunch is over we head to Mo Levitskys.

1st we walk down to the Garment District. The Garment District is fairly skanky anyway but Mo Levitskys is in the very skankiest part of it in this thin street that most people would never even look in and definitely would not buy clothes here. If you know where to go you go through this door and up 2 floors of dirty fucked up stairs and then through a glass door that says "Mo Levitskys" and you're in Mo Levitskys. It's basically 1 big room and there's so much stuff all over mostly racks of clothes and boxes you have to move sideways to go anywhere. Mo Levitskys is very cheap because Mo Levitsky gets everything straight from Korea where all the fancy stuff is made anyway I sometimes picture Mo Levitsky with a machine gun smuggling clothes out of Korea.

Mo Levitsky is a pretty old fairly portly guy and he's Jewish. Jews are very big in the Garment Trade. He has a Jewish accent (which my Dad doesn't) and he's nice in a "I'm so nice

because I want you to buy stuff" way. When we come in Mo
Levitsky comes up to my Dad and gives him this huge hand-
shake like he's the King Of England and says "Counselor!
Welcome!" and my Dad tries to be low key but you can tell
he's psyched so for the next practically an hour we try on
dress jackets and dress pants and shirts which is mostly work
type stuff for my Dad and for me things I could wear on nice
occasions or other wise. When my Dad sees something in my
size which is taller than his like a green shirt he brings it over
to me and I try it on and if my Dad likes it he nods and says
"Do you like it?" and I say "Yeah" or "No" and my Dad makes
me turn around and checks it all out and then I take it off and
we look for the defect which everyone has 1 because that's
1 reason it's so cheap at Mo Levitskys and we look around
until we find a little hole or a thread coming out usually somewhere you can't see it and unless it's something huge like a
sleeve missing my Dad nods and I nod. Sometimes my Dad
nods even if the sleeve is missing. Not really. But almost. Anyway everytime he likes something for him or me my Dad
takes it up to the front and Mo Levitsky says "Very sharp
Counselor very sharp" and then my Dad says how much and
Mo Levitsky says "15" or "20" and finally there's this whole
pile of stuff and they forget everything they said before and
Mo Levitsky just says "I'll give it to you for $300" meaning
everything and my Dad says "How about $150" and Mo Levit-
sky says "I have to make a living Counselor how about $270"
and my Dad says "Let's say $200" and Mo Levitsky says "Well
for you you're a good customer $250" and my Dad says "How
about $220?" and Mo Levitsky says "OK $240" and my Dad
says "OK."

I got a green button down shirt with a very very little hole in the underarm you couldn't see and a black blazer which if I were Christopher Lemon I would wear to school and a blue button down and a white button down shirt to wear with the blazer on dress occasions and 3 T-shirts made out of this very European material and a 10 pack of new socks.

So we walk back to my Dads office and then he goes back to work and I can go back to the train or wander around New York.

CHAPTER 14

OUR DAY IN THE CITY PART II
(SECRET ADDENDUM)

I don't know if I'm going to include this chapter in the book or not because I break laws and might get in legal trouble but Mr. Rasfenjohn always says "Write Everything rewrite later" so I'll write it and decide later. He also said just to me a couple times "Jeremy that which is true is noble and good" and what if he's right? (I'm not in Creative Composition this semester by the way because I can't take II until next year).

Anyway my Dad goes back to work and I wander around New York I don't really know where I'm going but maybe I'm going to Times Square where they drop the big Ball on New Years Eve and everything. They also have these dirty magazine etc. places which I have a healthy curiosity about so I just walk and I'm definitely having fun even though I don't know where I am because of not being in school and it's after school anyway and kids are everywhere and 1 thing I do is think about living in New York and hanging out with everybody going down the street and there are lots of groups of all black kids because a lot of black people live in New York. I thought about going and saying "What's up?" and hanging around New York with them and bringing them to Hutch Falls and introducing them to some of the white kids and some of the black kids there.

Anyway I see a bunch of non lit up neon signs and I realize I'm there a few blocks later the street is covered with Porno shops. It's very interesting. They've got "Private Viewing Booths" where for 25 Cents people go I think and sit in a booth and watch a movie or sometimes a naked lady dancing. There are also places with just doors and then places with huge guys out front saying stuff like "Check-Out the beautiful all naked ladies here" but they're bouncers too and they don't say anything to me because it's illegal for me to go in because I'm not 18. But I think it would be interesting to check out 1 of these places just to see what it's like and to learn. The 1st thing I realize is I have to go in a place with no guy out front who's going to card me and then some friend of my parents walks by and says "Jeremy Reskin what on Earth???" or maybe Mr. Bash (our next door neighbor) will come out of the store himself but at least then I can say "Well what are you doing here Mr. Bash??" if he says anything.

Anyway I go by a place where like the other places you can't see in and it says XXX MOVIES and SEX NOVELTIES and I look around and there are people on the street but no one really close or anything and I just go and push the door and go in.

1st of all there aren't a lot of people inside just 2 or 3. Everything's white like inside hospitals. There are magazines and videotapes and billions of Dildos which since I don't really suspect a lot of women go in here I don't know what anybody's doing with them. Right to my left is a glass case with lots of things in it and I'm curious to check it out but there's this Indian guy or something right behind the counter and he says "Too small!" I look at him and he looks at me and he says "Too small too small" and waves his hands around like he's crazy. "Huh?" I say but he says "You know too small 18 18" and he's pissed now and I just stand there like there's some big misunderstanding and I'm very very surprised and exasperated then he says "Too small!" again and I turn around and go back outside I walk pretty fast down the street and at least I know a lot more now about Dildos then I did 5 seconds before like there are a lot of them. I kind of wish Douglas was with me because he's good at stuff like this and doesn't care what anybody thinks about anything I don't think.

Anyway even though getting kicked out was a bummer I'm more into the whole thing now because it's like if you've shot-up Heroin once you might as well do it again because you've already done it once and what's the worse thing that could happen I could get thrown out again because I've learned now that's what they do it's not like they call the Cops or anything. I go in a couple more places but as soon as I go in I turn around and walk out just because I freak out slightly.

I noticed by the way a lot of times there are Indian guys and stuff like that working in porno shops I think because it's an opportunity for immigrants.

Anyway I keep going and a few blocks later I see "PLEASURE AND ECSTASY ADULT FANTASY SHOP" which sounds interesting so I go across the street and go in and this place has very bright lights inside too just like a hospital and is almost empty except for 1 fat American guy behind the counter eating. He doesn't look at me when I go in. I don't get thrown out.

I walk down an aisle with videos and check them out. Now I'm going to have to admit some things and I'm just going to go for it like the truth and cross it out later but after looking at about 1 box I have to admit I was kind of turned on because who wouldn't be even though this is kind of a gross place where you don't want to be. But the boxes have pictures on them with women looking very hot and wearing nothing or barely nothing sometimes just bras or very tight T-shirts stretched across their Tits so you can see through them and 1/2 their Tits are coming out the top anyway and then they're looking at you like they're really into you even though they don't even know you and basically I defy you to look at them for more than about 2 seconds without getting turned on.

So about 1/2 way down the aisle I realize at the end of the aisle there's another whole dark part of the store and I go look and this is where they've got "MOVIE BOOTHS" which I think means men basically going back there and letting it all hang out so to speak in a little room where let's just say you don't really want to walk around barefoot on the carpet or anything. I'm not totally sure what to do because I'm curious about the movies and want to learn about that too but the place is gross enough and the back part where all I'd have to do is go through this open door and turn to go there is just so super gross I don't go. Not to mention who knows what other perverts are back there waiting to maybe turn you into their own personal floor. If you know what I mean. Not that I can't take care of myself.

Anyway I go back down a different aisle where there are a million magazines. The magazines versus the videos are very different and the people on them include men and they've got these big red dots on the parts of the pictures where the woman is for example doing something to the man but some of them don't and you can basically see the whole thing. The magazines are kind of slimy looking, like the actual magazine is covered in slime or something and they're from all over the place not just America like Finland or Sweden or France and so the women in them are from Finland or Sweden or France and those women are more into sex than American women because they look like it's not even that big a deal to have these guys doing these things to them.

Anyway I want to get out of there in general and the best and least gross looking 1 of them because it's just got 1 pretty nice looking woman and a man on the front and she's giving him a Blow-job but it's partly but not completely dotted out by 1 of the dots is called FRENCH LUST and it's 1 of the foreign ones which maybe even makes it a little more like I'm buying art or something and I could say to my Dad "You said I should read more". Anyway I pick it up and I take it to the front and the guy is done eating now but I'm kind of grossed out he's touching my magazine because he's got Tuna Fish or something on his fingers even though I'm pretty psyched he's selling it to me without carding me or anything. I give him $7.99 and he puts it in a bag and gives it to me.

So I go outside.

I head for the train station. I look about 5000 times to see if you can see through the bag and even though you can't if you hold it up to the light and you're about a 10th of an inch away you can see the outline of the bottom of a naked Tit. I keep walking and finally I get on the train. Now I could know anybody on the train and I swear it's like the bag has basically huge letters on it that say "JEREMIAHS RAUNCHY FRENCH LUST PORNO HE JUST BOUGHT". Here's what I feel like: like I killed somebody for no reason and cut their head off with a chain saw and I've got the head in the bag. If I'd just brought my fucking back-pack it would just be in there and nobody would have a clue but I've got this brown paper bag from the Porno store and it's shaped like a magazine and it's just obviously what it is so I got ready if anybody says "What's in that bag?" to say "Sports Illustrated". I would probably see Renee at the train station in Hutch Falls and she'd say "hi Jeremy" and we'd talk for a second in Spanish and then she'd say "what's in your bag?" "Sports Illustrated". Then she'd say "Oh can I see it? There's this article I heard about." About some tennis player or something. And I'd say "Yeah but excuse me because I have to go kill myself."

Well I'm here today so I don't have to tell you Renee wasn't at the station. I took a cab home possible people who were home were my Mom who would look at the bag and instantly know what was in there because she's psychic about anything you don't want her to know so she'd be like "Jeremy is that issue number 62 of French Lust?" Beth who would yell "Mom Jeremy has this weird bag and I don't know what's in it" or "My womans intuition tells me Jeremys got dirty magazines" and that's it. Claire wouldn't say anything but it was like the

Nazis in there. Like Hogans Heroes but not funny so here's what I did.

I put the bag in my pants it wouldn't go down but I moved it to the side and it went down it was basically around my left leg so I had to keep it straight and kind of out in front of me to keep it from sliding all the way down. It didn't make a bulge really so I figured you couldn't notice it. I went in the door and there was the stairs and I could tell just from the atmosphere that Beth wasn't home but as soon as she heard the door like a vulture my Mom comes in from the kitchen and says "How was it?" "Fine" I said going to the stairs. "Did you go to the Deli?" Mom said. "Yeah Tannebaums." "How's your father?" "He's fine you'll see him in like 3 hours." I was up the 1st 4 stairs. "Why are you limping?" my Mom said. The magazine was slipping and I had to shoot my leg out to stop it I said "I'm not limping." "Did you hurt yourself?" "No." "Are you sure?" I was almost at the top and suddenly I said "I have a cramp" then I was around the corner and in my room.

I took the magazine out of the bag. The woman on the cover was this French girl with short black hair and medium-size Tits 1 of which was kind of swaying to the side because of the position she was in on her back with this French guy putting certain things in certain places but not necessarily the 1st place you think of if you know what I mean. The guy had a mustache and was pretty greasy like you figured he figured he was pretty lucky to get this job where all he had to do was stand there.

Inside at 1st there's a lot of pages with just writing in French and then all these ads for sex stuff and then I get to some pictures of this couple having intercourse. But it's not the couple from the cover it's some other French couple and they're both basically pretty ugly she's blond and has kind of extra stomach and just in no way is at all hot. She also has basically no Tits and he's even greasier and grosser than the guy on the cover and about the last thing I want to see is them. Which I see plenty of but I don't know who's looking at them. So I start going through the rest of the magazine and there's more French and then near the back more pictures specifically there are 2 women kissing and I'm like "where's the guy?" but at least they're not as ugly as the other couple even though they're not exactly Playboy material either. 1's tall with black hair and 1's short with black hair. Then there's some pictures of them doing different things all of which are like "Welllll" and then there's a picture of the 2 of them standing there and that's when I see it. The tall 1 has a Dick. I look away as fast as I can I think I might of yelled "Yeeeeeeuuuu-uccchhhh!" I was so grossed out I wanted to throw up all over my room and then I double-confirmed that the 1 with the dick had tits and was in fact a woman which she was. Or whatever she was.

French people are fucking sickos. That's all I have to say.

I slammed the magazine shut then I opened it again and checked out the rest just in case there was anything else there and there were some really good looking French women (with no dicks) doing stuff. There was also this story in French I didn't understand with some cartoons and then suddenly there's this part of it in english that has a cartoon of a man and woman having serious sex and she's sweating and she says in the balloon "messiuer please insert yourself" and when he does she says "Yes yes yes Oui oui oui Oh Ah."

Finally I closed the magazine forever I didn't know what to do with it. I thought about burying it in Nierbeck Woods but somebody could see me there even if I went way into the woods and think I was burying a dead body or something. I got a pen and a piece of paper from my desk and wrote this: TO WHOM IT MAY CONCERN: I BOUGHT THIS BY ACCIDENT. I DID NOT KNOW WHAT THE PICTURES INSIDE OF IT WERE. THEY TOTALLY GROSS ME OUT AND DO NOT TURN ME ON. I AM SORRY I BOUGHT IT. I opened the magazine again looking away so I didn't see anything I got to the page where the Woman with a Dick pictures start and I put the note there. Then I wrote an exact copy of the original note and taped it to the front of the magazine with scotch tape.

Then I got my box which locks out of the closet and the key out of my desk inside the box I've got some papers on top for sort of a diversionary manuver mostly stuff from 7th Grade I got good grades on then under all the papers I have a few Playboys. I read Playboy because I'm interested not just in seeing the pictures but in learning about the women and what kind of women do this kind of thing and stuff the 2 best are Elaine Driscoll who's from England and has red hair and medium-big Tits and she's at this castle in England taking a bath out front in basically this big steel bathtub that's more just a giant pot than a real bathtub she has this big sponge and she squeezes it over her Tits so she's got a lot of soap running down all over the place. And she's from England. Then the other best 1 is Gig Randall who I can most truthfully describe by saying she's got the biggest Tits in the world she's 23 because it probably took her at least that long to grow such big

Tits. And she's got black hair and she looks at you in this way like she's looking right at you her measurements are 39-24-36. With an emphasis on the 39. She's from this very big Italian family where they cook a lot together and everything. She seems kind of like a slut versus Elaine who judging from 1 of the pictures of her not naked in a bar hangs out with businessmen and that kind of people and dressed she's wearing this dress where you see more than just cleavage you can look down it and see 3/4 of her Tits. There's also Nanette Lutz who's a dental hygienist and there are pictures of her at this farmhouse facing 1/2 sideways and holding a piece of wood that's sticking out of the wall inside the barn to tie horses to or something and smiling and you can only see 1 Tit in the picture but the side view gets you to understand what it's like and she by the way has the biggest areolas ever and they're very bumpy too but so what. Also in the front pictures her Tits kind of hang down like they're very heavy and their shape is not just round but oblong. Which is different and makes her seem older and she's very white. Then there's Rory Neem who is basically just lame her hair is huge and greasy looking and kind of sticky-curly curly and she's super tall too tall for her non-Tits and her smile looks really fake I don't know how they picked her. Then there's Penthouse which is completely different the centerfold is named Sheila and she has this medallion hanging down between her Tits which are big kind of in every direction they really spread out and up and down and the medallion is really inbetween them down in there but the different thing about Penthouse is they totally show the vaginas. So Sheilas vagina is just basically on view it's hairy and she spreads it open so you can see inside and at 1st I was kind of like "Wow" then I got used to it. Penthouse is like a whole different thing. Like she's a very real woman. (Later Sheila won the Penthouse Pet Of The Year Award). Under that is Raquel Welch from the New Jersey Sentinel TV Section from about 4 years ago and it's a very little picture from that part where they show a little picture from a movie coming up that night called "1 Million Years B.C.". She's wearing this kind of cave man bikini where you can see her whole stomach and her legs and the bra part is pretty much nothing so you can see the entire tops of her famous Tits she's crouching down and she has this club in her hand like she's hunting or fighting someone. I'm really into Raquel Welch but 1 thing that's kind of weird is the picture's really old and she's like 50 now so that's weird because is it the past or the present and what does that all mean. Anyway under Raquel is an 8X10 glossy picture from a movie I never heard of called "The 60s" that I bought at a movie memorabilia store when I was in 7th Grade it's basically just a picture of a womans Tits with a T-Shirt stretched across them very very very tight and they're huge and the space inbetween them has these big wrinkles in the T-Shirt where it's being stretched by how big the Tits are and the T-Shirt says in big letters that are stretched too "COMELY". I used to like that word. And then under that was the cover of a book of my Moms called Fear Of Flying the cover is basically just a shot of this womans very huge cleavage in this sort of pose where she wants you to look at it. She's trying to turn you on you can't see her face or anything in the picture. I stole the book from my Moms shelf in my Mom and Dads room and ripped the cover off and kept it and burned the book in the kitchen sink when nobody was home in 6th

Grade. Don't burn things in the kitchen sink by the way. There's a lot of smoke and it doesn't all go away and you have to tell everyone later you burned some ravioli. Also if you burn a whole book it makes tons of ashes you have to get rid of you might as well have to get rid of the whole book. (Looking back now I don't know why I didn't just keep the whole book I was kind of an idiot.) So that's what's in the box. Anyway I put the magazine on the bottom face up so the note was the 1st thing you saw if anyone ever saw it and then I took 1 of the old English papers and put it on top of it because I didn't want to see it ever anymore either and then I put everything else back on top and locked the box and put it back in the closet.

I think the naked female form is a beautiful thing. Painters throughout history have painted it. In our society we're very nervous about people being naked but why? Also a naked beautiful female body in a museum is fine but in a magazine suddenly it's illegal. We should compromise and realize the body is beautiful. This more European attitude is good for society. Even though Europe includes France and they go too far.

CHAPTER 15

I SCREW UP BUT IT TURNS OUT OK
(CHAIN OF EVENTS)

Meanwhile back at school . . . me and Renee are getting pretty good at Spanish. We're still pretty spastic in class me especially but then 1 day in the hall she saw me when she was going by and she went "Ola". Without even thinking about it I went "Ola" she kept going and then the next day we passed each other and Renee suddenly said "Como estas?" and I right away went "Como Estas?" I think foreign languages just start to come naturally after a while. Anyway I didn't know what inspired all of this but there was a chain of events it started.

The 1st thing in the chain was 1 day the next week in Spanish 2nd Period when we were doing what Mr. Eller calls Social Vocabulary which is words like "novio" (which means boyfriend). He had us do a dialogue drill with the social vocabulary and Renee goes 1st and she says "Como esta su novia" (which means how is your girlfriend?) and I said "Bien" which means fine even though she probably knows I don't even have a girlfriend. Then I said "Como esta su novio" and Renee says "No tengo novio" (which means I don't have a boyfriend.) "Oh" I accidentally say and here's where the thing in the chain of events happened. I think because we'd been saying Ola in the hall and everything and also because in some weird way you just say stuff in Spanish (because it's not English) I say "Pero hombre en Rianeck?" (which means "But what about that guy from Rianeck") who I'd seen her with 1st Semester at the Rianeck Game. As soon as I said it I was like "Uh-oh what did I just say" Renee got this look I'd never seen her have before like she was very surprised and totally mad too like if I just said "Is Mr. Eller your novio" and he really was. Finally she says "No hombre en Rianeck No tengo novio." I wanted to say I'm really sorry and I didn't mean to say anything about that but I couldn't remember the Spanish for I'm sorry and I didn't know the rest of it so I didn't say anything and then Mr. Eller says "Termine Dialogue".

Class was over and Renee packed up her stuff and went out fast.

#2 in the chain of events: I'm going down the hall after 5th Period and I see Renee and she's wearing this light blue tight sweater with a V at the top where you see her lower neck and the skin all over there on her chest (not her Tits though) and she looks hot and pretty at the same time and she's coming right up to me and she stops and says "I need to talk to you." "OK" I say. "Can you talk after school?" "Yeah" I said. "Meet me at the tables outside the Lunchroom?" "OK" I said.

Here are the things I figured might happen - 1. John

McKnight and Randy Brewer and 1/2 the guys in the Sopho-more class and 1/2 the guys in the Senior class would be there and they'd pretty much beat me to death. And Renee would be going "Kick his fucking ass!" or maybe the guy from Ria-neck himself would be there and he'd be like "hey man why are you rubbing your nose in Renees business?" Or maybe Renee would be alone and she'd say "I know I was nice to you saying Ola in the hall and everything but my <u>real</u> life is none of your business maybe if you had a novio of your own you wouldn't be so interested in other peoples lives." I didn't think these things would actually happen it's just stuff I think about. So 6th Period Bio II was a pretty sucky 45 minutes thinking about it all and not listening to Mr. Tapp talking about cells.

Anyway I go to the courtyard after class is over and when I get there she isn't there winter is pretty much over but it's still 1 of those days when the weather's like "fuck you" because in the morning it's nice and you go to school in a sweater but then you get out of school and it's freezing and this wet rainy slush is coming down from the sky and big slush puddles are everywhere so I'm standing there in the courtyard next to the door to the Lunchroom like an idiot in wet sneakers and no jacket and I'm freezing and wet like a wet dog. Finally I see Renee coming up and she's in this Dick Tracy overcoat with a belt tied in a knot in front and rubber Duck Boots so she can stand around all day if she wants to and her hair is wet and it's less straight when it's wet and with that and the coat and everything she's so beautiful and could I'm sure easily be 23. When I see her I get really nervous and it's stupid but I totally want to marry her.

She comes up right next to me and says "Thank you for coming."

"Sure" I say.

"Jeremy how did you know about David?" She's whispering even though there isn't a single person anywhere.

I say "I didn't really know I just saw you guys once at the Rianeck game."

"Oh God" she said.

"I didn't see anything just you guys standing there."

Really I saw them having a big fight and his hand on her shoulder but I didn't say that.

"What were you doing back there?"

"I was just walking around at half-time I wasn't looking for you or anything."

"Oh God" Renee said and she looked at this big puddle next to us full of water that was getting fuller all the time her hair was getting wetter and it was really dark now like if she had black hair and water was dripping off it.

"Sorry" I said.

"Who did you tell?"

"Nobody."

"Really?"

"I swear."

"Did you tell John or Randy?"

"No."

"You didn't tell them in the locker room?"

"No I swear I never even talk to those guys especially since soccers over."

"Jeremy I want you to tell me the truth no matter what it is did you tell anybody?"

"No not even my Mom."

Well that pretty much stopped the conversation I couldn't believe I said it it wasn't like I ever ever tell my Mom anything about school but now it sounded like I was totally a Mommas boy and I tell her everything. I just said my Mom because it was someone I know really well to prove a point that I wouldn't even tell somebody like that.

"I mean I don't tell my Mom"

"It's OK" Renee said.

"No but I mean"

"I know" she said.

I wanted to explain but I could tell it would just make it worse.

"Why's it so bad if people know?" I said.

"We're not going out anymore" Renee said "so it's not true."

"Oh" I said.

She looked down at that puddle again and she kicked her boot in it and it splashed on me.

"Oh sorry" Renee said.

"That's OK."

I was so wet it didn't matter anyway Renee put her hands in her Dick Tracy coat pockets and said "the thing is that David's a great guy but he's not friends with John and Randy."

"Oh" I said.

Then she said "I'd just moved here all my friends were in Japan. I really wanted to be friends with those guys."

"But they would of been friends with you."

"Guys are - well - with John and Randy they just wouldn't of been friends with me if I had a boyfriend."

"Really?" I said.

"Absolutely."

"Are you sure?"

"Yes."

"I think they would" I said.

"Do you think?"

"Yeah."

Renee looked around a little.

"You're naive Jeremy."

I didn't say anything then I said "I think your friends are your friends no matter what."

"That's my point" she said and she sounded mad. "They weren't my friends."

"Well they are now" I said.

"I know but if Jeremy if it turned out I was lying I don't want them to think I'm a liar."

"Mmm-hmm" I said.

"Besides Lenea had a crush on him too. I didn't want her to be hurt."

We stood there and then I said "where do you know him from?"

"He goes to RTS I met him at a party."

"Oh" I said.

"He's a great guy."

"Why'd you break up with him?"

"What makes you think I broke up with him?"

"Um. I don't know."

"We were fighting a lot. It was a destructive relationship for both of us."

"Oh" I said.

I was so wet now that I was almost shivering and Renee said "You're all wet."

"I know" I said.

"Well Jeremy." And she stopped for a second then she said "Thank you. For not telling anyone. A lot of guys would of they can't mind their own business."

"That's OK" I said.

For a millisecond I thought she was going to hug me or kiss me (in a friends way) but then she just turned around and walked away. She was going in the only direction there was so I had to wait there standing in the rain until she turned around the side of the building and then got a little further away so I wouldn't run into her when I went.

That night after talking to Renee I was lying in bed when I fell asleep. I had insomnia and I kept waking up and falling asleep and having different dreams. In the main 1 I remember I dreamed I was flying to Mount Kilimanjaro. (This mountain is in Africa if it exists which I think it does). I'm flying a plane towards this huge mountain with snow all over it like a giant snowcone. The snow is flying back and forth. Renee is next to me and I'm not sure but I think she's the co-pilot. I've never flown a plane in real life but in the dream when I pull the steering thing up the plane starts to go up and when I pull it down it goes back down and it feels so real it's like I'm really in a plane that's moving as I fly it and it feels totally like reality. It was definitely the most realistic dream I ever had. Even though nothing else happened.

I think this dream was inspired by the Ernest Hemingway short story The Snows Of Kilimanjaro but in Hemingways story the dream is different. The main character (who probably represents Hemingway) is dying of a leg infection and he goes on a plane ride back to civilization to get to a hospital even though it's probably already too late.

Then they began to climb and they were going to the East it seemed, and then it darkened and they were in a storm, the rain so thick it seemed like flying through a waterfall, and then they were out and Compie turned his head and grinned and pointed and there, ahead, all he could see, as wide as all the world, great, high, and unbelievably white in the sun, was the square top of Kilimanjaro. And then he knew that there was where he was going.

But we discover later it's all a dream and really he's dreaming this while he's dying and then he dies.

Outside the tent the hyena made the same strange noise that had awakened her. But she did not hear him for the beating of her heart.

I've noticed people die at the end of stories all the time.

I bet Renee had a dream that night too but with me in it only as a minor character or not at all. I bet it was a night of magic and everyone in Hutch Falls dreamed something about somebody.

CHAPTER 16

GILLIAN MAKES HER MOVE

"**H**ello?"

"It's Caroline I need you at the theater right now."

"What's wrong?"

"Just get over there right now."

"OK."

It was Friday night and we all had plans for Saturday night so I was home doing nothing. Beth was home and Mom asked her to drive me and she did but she was kind of weird in the car like she was thinking about something. Drivers Ed started in February and it was a piece of cake and I was an excellent driver so I wouldn't be stuck with her driving me forever but even after I get my permit I can't drive alone until I turn 16 which is after summer vacation starts so that sucks.

Anyway the theater we go to in Hutch Falls is by the mall but off in its own place you turn right at Long John Silvers and go down this road and there it is. Everyone hangs out in back where there's extra parking and this wall to sit on that goes all the way around the parking lot like they put it there for people to sit on. It's dark back there and people from different schools sit in different parts but it's not like a rule where you sit you just go to any open place and sit there with your friends when they get there.

Previously I told my Dad I needed a leather jacket because I didn't want to wear my soccer jacket all year like I did last year and I didn't want to wear my down jacket when it wasn't freezing. So I figured my Dad would find like the Mo Levitskys of leather jackets and take me there but he came home 1 day with a big bag and inside the bag was a leather jacket. It had big strips going down both sides and then inside the strips where you didn't really know they were there were pockets. My Dad said "It's a European style". I thought it looked weird but when I put it on I liked it I wore it all night and even lay down in bed in it but I didn't sleep in it because I'm not an idiot. It smelled great like fresh leather and OK I admit it about 50 times I looked in the mirror and went "Eeeyyyy" like The Fonz. Anyway with my jacket it was cool behind the theater now because even if I didn't smoke or anything I had it and it looked cool so nobody was going to fuck with me or think what the fuck is he doing here.

In fact when I didn't see Caroline instead of going back around the front and waiting in front for her where a lot of people were waiting for movies and people I wandered around and then staked out an area on the wall and just stood there.

Finally I see Caroline she's in 1 of her tight sweaters (the white 1) and has a purse around her shoulders so the strap is down right between her Tits and kind of presses the sweater down over the Tits so you can really see them. She's also got these 60s Jeans she wears sometimes that make her look like a drugged out hippie freak. She comes towards me and you can tell something's really wrong by the expression on her face.

"Hey" I say.

"I can't fucking believe this" she said.

"What?" I say.

"My crazy insane freak bitch mother."

"What about her."

"She kicked me out."

"Of the house?"

"Yes."

"Really?"

"Yes."

"When?"

"Now."

"Why?"

"She's a complete lunatic."

"What happened?"

"She found out about Rich."

"I thought she knew about him."

"She did but she didn't know how old he was."

"She never met him?"

"No."

"How'd she find out?"

"She asked him."

"Oh."

When she's talking she's so freaked out she isn't even smoking (which is like Uh-oh something's really wrong).

"We got in a huge fight. I was like Richie's a great guy and it doesn't matter what age he is. Then she wants to know did we have sex which is none of her fucking business." She put both of her hands on her waist and she said "She said he was a pervert." She looked at me. "So I said you're a pervert. Then we started screaming and she kicked me out!"

"What did she say?" I said.

"She said Get Out."

"What like forever?"

"Yes."

"She probably didn't mean forever."

"She kicked me out."

"She was probably just upset."

"I can't believe this I can't fucking believe she kicked me out."

"She probably just thought you'd both be better off with some time alone. You know to cool off?"

"I hate her."

"No you don't."

"And she hates me."

"No she doesn't Caroline your Mom loves you."

"Jeremy Jeremy" she said twice and then she stopped for a second and said "God."

"Do you want to call her?" I said.

"No."

"Maybe you should call her and try to make up. Maybe she just meant get out for right now for like an hour or 2 so she can be alone."

Now she went into her purse and got a cigarette then she rooted around in her purse some more but she couldn't find a match. She went over to this group of girls some of who were smoking on the wall got a light from 1 and came back. She was standing there taking a lot of puffs when I saw Douglas walking across the parking lot.

I was sort of surprised because I kind of thought the way Caroline said I need you to come to the theater right now like it's some big emergency she wanted to talk to me immediately and it had to be fast because it was just me and I was kind of like "Hmmm" when I saw Douglas but not because I was jealous or wanted Caroline or anything that wasn't it I didn't want Caroline.

I was so into Renee and Caroline also didn't look as good as last year when I was a little into her she was kind of getting older looking and just life I think was taking a toll on her now.

So Douglas comes up and the 1st thing he gives Caroline this big hug and she's holding her cigarette behind his back when they're hugging and she says to him "My Mom kicked me out."

"What a Cunt" Douglas says.

"Out of the house" Caroline said.

"She's psychotic."

"Well why did I have to get a psycho mom?"

"You got screwed on fathers too" Douglas said.

Caroline actually laughed when he said this then they sat down on the wall and they were talking to each other and I'm like why is she so psyched to see Douglas when he's like Your Mom's a cunt.

Pretty soon after that Gillian and Kath got there so now the whole gang was here. Gillian and Caroline went off to talk and Kath who does this sometimes looked at me and said "Drama drama drama."

Meanwhile when Gillian and Caroline go off Douglas says "Hi".

"Hey" I said.

"She's flipping out" he said.

"Yeah" I said.

"Her Mom's a bitch."

"She doesn't seem like that."

"What do you mean?"

"She seems OK."

"That's because you're there. It's different when people are over. Aren't your parents different when people are over?"

"Not really."

"Mine are."

"Oh."

"That's why I never have people over."

The girls came back and Gillian said "Let's go to my house". Douglas drove. Gillians Mom was watching TV and we didn't say hi we just went right down to the basement Caroline was in this really weird mood now not freaking out as much but very quiet and I was actually pretty worried about her. Douglas was putting his arm around her and sitting next to her on the floor and he was whispering stuff in her ear Kath told this really long story about how her Mom had forced her to go on this diet when she was in 5th grade and she got really sick and had to go to the hospital and how her Mom said to the Doctor "Well what am I supposed to do about her weight?" when Kath was sleeping only Kath wasn't sleeping she was just lying there and the whole thing was kind of im-plicating "Caroline you're not the only 1 with a fucked up Mom and problems" but in this Kath way and don't think Caroline got it because she just said "Bummer" after the story and went back talking to Douglas.

And now here's what happened next. Douglas and Caroline are sitting there and they're whispering and then they just get up and go in the guest bedroom which has wood paneling and a bed and sheets and stuff. Now maybe they were just going because Caroline was freaking out and needed to be alone or maybe he was going to give her a backrub but why couldn't they do it here and then right after Kath suddenly says "I'm really tired I'm going home" (it's like 8:30). And she just goes right upstairs and calls her mom and goes.

So now it's me and Gillian I'm on the brown couch and she's on the floor sitting and she gets up and sits down on the couch.

"Poor Caroline" she says.

"Yeah. She doesn't know how to deal with stuff like this" I say.

"I suppose" said Gillian. "But she'll be OK."

"You think?"

"Oh I don't know. Don't you think?"

"Not really."

"Look at all she's gone through. With her Dad. Those things make you stronger."

We sat there for a while and you couldn't hear anything from the other room where Douglas and Caroline were and I was just spacing out when suddenly I feel Gillians hand on my arm and she was right next to me and she says "Jeremy?"

She was practically whispering.

"Yeah?"

"Well" she said and she looked down for a second then she looked up but not right at me and she started to move her face towards me and I said "What's going on with them?"

Gillian said "Douglas and Caroline?" And she took her hand off me.

"Yeah I mean what's Douglas doing?"

"I don't know I guess he's I guess he's,"

"I mean she's really hurt right now" I said.

"Oh she's like this 1/2 the time anyway."

"Not this bad."

"I suppose."

"He's being a jerk I don't care what he thinks he's supposed to be being her friend now."

"Oh it's not such a big deal."

"Yes it is."

"People need each other Jeremy."

I was going to get up but it seemed weird but then Gillian got up and she went upstairs.

Caroline and Douglas came out of the room a little while later.

"Where's Gillian?" Caroline said.

"Upstairs."

Caroline went upstairs and Douglas stood there in front of the couch he just stood there sort of smiling then he sat down next to me on the couch.

"She's really great" he said.

"Uh-huh" I said.

"She's so, innocent. Under all that stuff. Man. Wow."

"Is she OK?" I said.

"No she's all fucked up but then she forgot it all. I think I'm in love with her."

"You're not in love with her" I said.

He looked at me.

"How do you know?"

"I don't know know I just think it's a bad situation."

He said "She's so sweet. The way she is."

"Yeah" I said.

I was pretty freaked out that night I didn't talk to Gillian again I just sort of waved goodbye when we left but when I went to bed I felt really weird like something happened to my life. I know she sort of made a pass at me I wasn't stupid. And I knew Douglas was in about the best mood of his life I wasn't jealous that he was with Caroline and I wasn't. I swear but I think I felt worried about Gillian and my friendship with her there wasn't really anything to say about it. I couldn't call her and say "what happened?" I just sleep in my underwear and I was lying there on the bed thinking and wondering about it.

CHAPTER 17

CHAIN OF EVENTS

I didn't know there would be 3 things in the chain of events but there are. Thing #3 in the chain of events: If you're on a team you get out of class early for away games. It's basically the best moment of your life you're sitting there in some boring class and pretty much wanting to set yourself on fire and die and then about 20 minutes before you're really supposed to go you look around at the other guys on the team and then someone says "Mr. Or Mrs. Whatever the soccer team has to go." The cool teachers like Mr. Rasfenjohn are like "Have a good game" but most of the teachers make this face like what kind of sick people think sports are more important than this boring fucking class but they don't stop you because they can't versus Mr. Rasfenjohn who would want you to play soccer even if he had a choice because he believes people should express themselves and do what they want. For example 1 day 1st Semester Greg Elbet was writing a paragraph about his dog and he said his dad said "this is fucking absurd" when he was talking to the Vet about the dog dying and could he put that in the story and Mr. Rasfenjohn said yes you can express yourself anyway you want but don't tell your parents or I'll be in trouble. Not to mention writing anything you want about sex. 1 time a girl named Tanya Laroach wrote a story about this guy she was so in love with and how he ignored her then later he liked her and how they basically had sex for the 1st time (or almost sex) in this dark room and Mr. Rasfenjohn said "That was excellent". Anyway then not only are you going to a soccer game but you're not in class too so you're totally psyched. So of course this hasn't happened to me since soccer ended but it was still happening to the baseball team on which John McKnight and Randy Brewer were. And 1 day when my last period class was gym I went down to the locker room in the middle of gym to go to the bathroom and the baseball team was down there changing and when I was going by them John McKnight goes "Jeremy!"

"Hey" I said.

"What's up Man?"

"I got gym" I said.

"You oughta be playing baseball we just got outa bio."

"Yeah" I said.

"Seriously man you oughta play baseball" Randy said.

"I guess" I said.

I sucked at baseball.

I had to go back to gym but then John said "you're in Spanish with Renee right?"

"Yeah" I said.

"That's cool" John said.

"She's fucking smart" Randy said.

"Yeah" I said. "I mean she didn't speak any Spanish at the beginning of the year and now she's like fluent."

"She speaks Japanese too" Randy said.

"Yeah" I said.

"Well think about baseball man" John said.

"OK" I said.

They left.

"Catch you later" John said.

"OK" I said.

Now you may ask why is that in the chain of events. Well I'm not sure but I think Renee said something to them about me after we talked after school that day like "that Jeremy guy who was on the soccer team with you guys is in my Spanish class" or maybe because I didn't tell anyone about the David guy she said "he's cool." But I don't really know.

Anyway the next day Renee goes by me in the hall and she stops but she really stops this time totally and stands next to me like she's not going anywhere and says in English "Hi Jeremy."

"Hey Renee" I say.

And she just talked for like 2 minutes about crap like Mr. Shipp who got sort of skimmed by a bus but was OK and other stuff and then we had to go to class and we go. But it's like suddenly I'm talking to everybody.

Then that same day at lunch I went out to the balcony and Caroline wasn't even there and Kath of course was sick and it was just me and Douglas and Gillian and everyone was just munching away on their sandwiches and no one was saying much but I swear Douglas was munching a little more happily than he used to since his night with Caroline and even though nothing's really happened with it as far as I know no one's said anything to me about it except Kath who a few days before when we went to throw our garbage away said "So what do you think?" in this really "Weeellll" way and I just said "What are you talking about?" even though I knew what she was talking about was Caroline and Douglas. So we're sitting there without much talking and I wondered about what would happen if Mr. Hallen the Principal came out when we were all there and Caroline and Gillian were smoking away and he said "This is very serious" and I went up to him and said "Mr. Hallen a word with you" and we went over against the railing where nobody could hear us and I'd say "Listen we're just hanging out out here we're not killing anybody or anything why don't you just go back inside and forget about it" and I would give him this look like "You want to do what I say" and he'd say "OK Jeremy" and I'd just sit back down with them and be like "don't worry about it". I also thought about us at a movie in the parking lot sitting on the brick wall and it got really windy and everybody was being swept away and up into the trees and getting hurt and everything and leafs were everywhere and it got very cold then this huge beam came down and started pulling Gillian and Douglas and Caroline and Kath upwards and it didn't get me but when I saw what was happening I ran and jumped and grabbed Douglas and I got his leg and I had him but the force was too strong and it tore him away and all of them were going up unable to fight the power of the beam and with the looks on their faces of fear and also yellow because of the beam and then I dove into the beam myself so I went up behind them. We get up into the ship and because I came later and they weren't expecting me no-body knows I'm there so I hide behind this rafter and watch these brown aliens talking to each other like "Aaza wzaa" and then they take everybody away somewhere and I can't follow without being detected so I explore the ship for a while which has a lot of levels and is very cool. It's dark on the ship and also you can hear the thump of footsteps far and close on the steel floors and hear water dripping. There is a good alien named Pizar who I meet when he whispers "Hissss" at me as I'm going by in the hall and I slip into the storeroom with him here you can really hear the water dripping Pizar explains that his people are going through a bad period of history doing evil things and not respecting humanity but there are good ones fighting to restore things. Later I crawl through a chute and I find the room where they've got everybody but I can't get in there's this very thick glass door so I look through and there's everybody sitting around on the floor looking sad and freaked out and Caroline who's smoking a cigarette. I bang on the door as hard as I can but they can't hear me and nobody sees me then I hear a guard coming so I go away qui-etly. Much later but not as much later as you might think we land everyone leaves the ship and my friends are led off. I wait until it's dark then I sneak off I find a place to hide and I sleep until I wake up. When I get up I see the planet for the 1st time it's like Earth except it's hotter and has a red sun. I go into the town and some aliens see me and don't do anything so I stop hiding as much the aliens don't all look like the ones on the ship they are every shape and size so I'm not as easy to no-tice. I remember Pizar telling me his people can change into any shape they want which is why they all look different and

I realize they probably just think I changed into this shape. That night I go to the town square and Gillian and Caroline and Douglas and Kath are there on exhibit basically dead in these beds covered with glass tops and I see them all lying there looking very white and dead. I'm depressed and I find a bar and have this green drink that's gross but strong and feels good I start talking to these 2 alien women who are hideous and ugly but seem impressed by the shape I thought of and turn themselves into beautiful women who look a little like Raquel Welch and Bo Derek but not too much to be realistic. We go for a walk in the dark down at this red river where nobody else is around and soon 1 thing leads to another I'm a little grossed out by what they were a second ago but there's no trace of it or anything and finally I forget who they really are and just enjoy that they're women now. When they go home I go to the castle in the middle of town where the rulers live it's heavily guarded but I climb this wall in back and get in a window. I run into a few guards and get in a fight with them and it turns out even though they are fast and tough and strong and can hit you hard and beat the crap out of you and send you flying across the room you can if you do it right I learn from trial and error rip their arms off by twisting them hard and blood goes blasting out of their shoulders and arms and I use some of their own arms to hit them with in the fight. Anyway I find their supreme leader in this big room and he's like "Who art thou?" and I say Jeremiah Reskin from Earth and he says "We did not take you" and I ignore him and I just say "those are my friends out there". He says "Your human loyalty is pitiful and impressive". I say "We're different from you but that doesn't mean you have the right to beam us up and kill us without warning and take us to your alien zoo or whatever it is" we argue for a while then he says "Jeremiah Reskin I have decided to honor your request to spare your friends lifes and return all of you to your planet. Also I honor you and if you would like to come back and visit our planet and its whole solar system we will bring you back and you may live among us as 1 of us for as long as you like. It will be interesting." He also mentioned they can change shape and looks and every-thing and turn into beautiful human women and I was like I know. Then I said "by the way do you think you could pro-gram Caroline to stop smoking" and he was like no we're not allowed to meddle in the affairs of other races. I was like suck-ing us up from our planet and killing us isn't meddling? but I didn't say anything.

Anyway the sacred process for bringing them back to life involves me we go out to the town square where they all are laid out in a circle and I have to put my hand on the glass tops while the aliens use their powers to funnel some of my human life force back into them. Their eye lids flutter. They're still basically asleep on the trip home but when we get there we beam back down and Gillian and Caroline and Douglas and Kath wake up and they're like "Wo what happened". And I'm like "Nothing everybody's OK". The storm and blowing wind from the ship was over and we walked away.

When I was thinking about this I ate my sandwich and nobody was talking. I guess I think about some weird shit sometimes. But so what? Everybody does. Probably. I think everybody has an imagination and uses it to think about things. I might think about space for example because I just like space and it's the last frontier. Nothing's known and everything's possible. Gillian I'm sure thinks about the perfect guy for her and ultimate love and finding happiness. Kath probably thinks about being thin. Caroline thinks about being with Pink Floyd somewhere. Douglas thinks about ruling the world his way and making everything make sense. John McKnight probably thinks about being John McKnight.

CHAPTER 18

THE FAN GETS HIT BY SHIT

Here's how I personally would describe things since "the night" with Gillian - screwed-up. Everyone obviously found out about it because 1 of the Laws of Physics is how secret something is corresponds inversely to how fast everyone finds out about it and I could tell everyone just knew and was freaked out. Especially with Gillian it's like she's different and I think everyone else too is even though I don't know why Caroline or Kath are different because of what happened with me and Gillian unless they're different because of solidarity with her or Caroline's different because of what happened with her and Douglas. But Douglas is the same as always I guess I can count on Douglas for that - for always being the same no matter what. I talked to him about all of it when we went to my house 1 day after school to hang out.

"I can't figure her out" he said.

"Caroline?"

"Yes."

"Oh" I said.

"I don't know what she wants 1 night she's all over me and the next night she's frigid as hell."

"Well did you guys you know."

"Sort of."

"Yeah?"

"But not exactly."

"Other stuff though."

"Lots of other stuff."

"A lot of times or what?"

"Not really that's what I'm saying."

"Oh."

"There was that 1 night and then she's just frigid a lot."

"She's not back with Richie is she?"

"Her Mom won't let her her Mom wants her to be with me."

"That's bad."

"I know."

"It's optimal if the parents hate you."

"VTS I should burn her house down or something."

I said "I think it's a Law Of Physics the more the parents like you the less the girl likes you."

"Agree" said Douglas.

"What's up with you and Gillian?" he said.

"Nothing" I said.

"Seems like something."

"It may seem like something but things aren't always what they seem."

"Do you want something to be up?"

"No not really."

"I thought you did."

"I never said I was into Gillian."

"True but you never said you weren't."

"I have to say I'm not into someone or I'm into them? Do you think I'm into every girl in the world?"

"Just about" said Douglas.

"Very funny."

I thought about telling him about Renee but I felt too stupid because he'd be like "Yeah right". Douglas insists that everything in the world be a fact and obvious plus he looks down on people like Renee because he can't see past the fact that they're popular and probably think they're cool even though as we've seen Renee doesn't think that she's more just normal and worried about herself.

I said "I'm not into Gillian other than you she's like my best friend."

"You don't want to screw that up."

"Yeah."

"Unless she had bigger Tits then you would."

"Fuck you" I said.

"Remember when we were all just friends?"

"Yeah."

"I miss the simpler times like 6th grade? That was a simple time."

"VTS" I said.

I wasn't mad at Douglas anymore about Caroline I felt sorry for him. I could tell he was badly hurt even though he would never admit it. And that maybe he was in love with her after all.

So things are normal and not normal normal because we're hanging out just like before but not normal because it's all weird. I mean on Friday or Saturday night we still go to Gillian or Carolines or a movie or to the Food Court but it's just weird.

Anyway 1 night we're at Gillians which is obviously where it all happened in the 1st place. We're all there Caroline I think is stoned and she's the only 1 and she didn't say anything to anyone about doing it so she must have just got stoned alone which is bad news of the know when your friends are screwed up by the school psychologist kind and she's off in her own little world and I'm next to Gillian on the brown couch because I'm trying to do what I would be doing even if everything was normal versus acting weird and making everything weirder by not talking to her or something like that and Douglas and Kath are talking on the other couch and Gillian just suddenly says:

"Jeremy what's going on here?"

"What do you mean?" I say.

"You know with us."

"I don't know" I say.

"Yes you do."

She's talking in this normal voice so I don't think anyone else knows we're talking about it.

"What do you thinks going on?" I said.

"So you do know somethings going on?"

I fell into her trap.

"I I don't know. Nothings going on. With me personally. Nothing. What do you think?"

"Have an idea for yourself Jeremy" Gillian said.

That was harsh.

"I have ideas all the time" I said.

"I suppose" said Gillian.

"Well what's going on with you?"

"Jeremy you're so. You're impossible everything isn't such a big deal you don't have to create a big deal out of every little thing."

"I don't create a big deal out of every little thing."

"You do you really do. Everything doesn't have to mean something."

"I know."

"People can just, do things. It's not always so important."

"I know" I said.

We sat there for a while and then Gillians mood changed she seemed so sad or full of memories or nostalgia now.

"You're a wonderful man Jeremy" she said.

"Thanks" I said.

"So don't forget that."

"You're a great person" I said.

"I suppose. But just remember. Be true to yourself that's your challenge. Your weakness Jeremy your Achilles Heel you're not always true to yourself."

I didn't say anything. Then Gillian said "Just always be Jeremy all the time. Because if you do - if you do - then your heart will shine some day Jeremy."

I didn't really know what she meant but I thought about it a lot later and even though I'm still not sure I think it's important to listen to your friends like Gillian when they're talking about you and try to be a better person. I said "I will". "Try" she said. "Yeah" I said.

But everything was different.

CHAPTER 19

BASEBALL

I decided on the spur of the moment to go to a baseball game. It was the 1st 1 I ever went to because 1st of all we don't have a baseball field at school so they play at Baileys Farm (which isn't a farm it's a place with baseball fields) and you have to go there and 2nd of all since I was about 8 (before then I liked baseball) I hate baseball. Because it's so boring. In soccer stuff happens the balls always moving and you don't stop every 2 seconds and that's why it's fun and exciting. Baseball should be called "Standing Around Ball". Boring with a capital Snore.

A bus goes after school to Baileys Farm for home games or wherever they're going for away games and I was just walking through the parking lot going home and then before I knew it I was on the bus. Like I went through the Star Trek transporter and there I was without knowing it. There were only about 5 people on it because 1st of all nobody goes to baseball games and 2nd of all everybody gets rides. Anyway we go out to Beane Municipal Park which is distant where some schools have their home games because this isn't a home game and there's about 5 games going on and 1 has a lot of fans because I guess at some schools they don't know baseball sucks and each field has bleachers next to it and this is where the fans from Hutch Falls are sitting by the Hutch Falls game not very many of them. The teams are warming up and they start the game.

I go over and stand by the bleachers and I look around and I immediately see Renee and Lenea and Cindy in the middle of the stands (upwise) and the middle (sidewise) then there's a bunch of other people around in different places and a few teachers so I just sort of stand there which is cool because other people are standing around too and people are coming and going and also just because there's so many people around from other schools because of all the games including Bedford South which is sort of a minor rival for us and Willdon which I don't know anything about and who knows who's who and what's going on. So I'm cool just standing there and I watch the 1st couple innings by the way it's pretty warm and fortunately not raining and the sun's going down but it's nowhere near all the way down so it's not hot it's just sort of perfect and beautiful. What a great day.

I try not to look a lot at Renee because 1 of the truest Laws Of Physics is that if you look a lot you will get busted. Not that they'd be looking at me but they could be looking in the general direction of me and then accidentally bust me looking at them plus now that Renee really knows me pretty well maybe she might look at me for a second and think "there's Jeremy Reskin from Spanish."

Which is sort of what happens but in reverse. It's the 3rd inning we're losing 2 to nothing John McKnight by the way has struck out twice and you can see he's getting pissed we're playing Weston-Barley which is a very working class school from Weston and Barley so they're good at sports and they come up to bat in the 3rd inning. I look around for no particular reason and then I look over around Renee and then I notice her head is pointing in the direction of me versus looking at the field and instead of looking away I can't stop I look right at her and she's looking right at me and she waves. And I wave except what my hand actually does is kind of a retarded 1/2-wave and then she waves again but this 1 looks like a "Come Here" wave and because my mind has a mind of its own totally without meaning to I do that thing where you look around like you think the person is talking to a person standing there behind you and then Renee laughs and points her finger at me like she's saying "No you moron!"

So I start to go. I go up into the bleachers and then I'm right next to Renee.

"Hi Jeremy" she says.

"Hey" I say. "What's up?"

"Sit down" she commands and I sit down next to her.

"Good game" I say.

"Oh it's so boring" she says.

"Yeah" I say.

"John struck out twice" she said.

"Yeah" I said. "That guy can pitch."

"What?" Renee said.

She was watching the game and not looking at me.

"Nothing I just said he was a good pitcher."

"Number 17 has a cute butt" Cindy said.

She was talking about a guy on the other team. Renee Lenea and Cindy were all drinking Tabs then Renee kind of 1/2 looked at me and said "Do you want a Tab?"

"No thanks" I said.

"I do like that butt" Lenea says.

"Jeremy you know Lenea and Cindy don't you?" Renee said to me.

Suddenly I realized I didn't know if I knew them or not I mean of course I knew who they were but I'd probably never said anything to them so "Yes" and "No" were both kind of not true and also might seem not true and bother them but I saved my own ass by suddenly just saying "Hey".

"Hi" "Hi" they both said.

"Jeremy's the genius of our Spanish class" Renee said and for a second I wasn't sure if she was serious or joking and also then if maybe I wasn't as bad at Spanish as I thought but then she laughed not in a mean way in a way like it was just a little joke and I laughed and I said "I'm pretty good but Renee is totally fluent" and we both laugh and then Lenea said "I should of taken Spanish French is a waste of time nobody speaks French."

"They do in France" Renee said which was funny because it was funny and also because Renee lived in Japan and went around the world so she knew more about that kind of thing (Not that you have to know that much to know they speak French in France.)

"Jeremy do you play on the soccer team?" Lenea said.

"Yeah" I said.

"I thought so you play in the back right?"

For a second I didn't know what she meant then I realized she meant I was a fullback.

"Yeah" I said.

"You guys sucked this year" Cindy said.

"Yeah I guess we did" I said.

Let me describe what Cindy was wearing it was warm and she's got this very very very curly blond hair and she's wearing this purple shirt that's shiny but the key thing is the top 3 or 4 or 5 buttons are unbuttoned so even though Cindy always had medium to medium-small size Tits suddenly when she leaned over to say something or something you could basically almost see them not quite everything but a big chunk of the tops and her bra too which was black by the way and also I think maybe they'd been growing but either way they were like "Wo" and then also the looking down-in factor. Even though I was in love with Renee and thought about her all the time when I saw Cindy in the hall or now I really liked her she had sexy hair. Lenea was different 1st of all she had black hair and no curls and her skin was very very dark so she looked kind of like she was Greek or something like Claire and then her face is sort of tall. What she looked like was 1 of those totally-grown-up models in their 30s in an ad for pantyhose or something walking down the street and the winds blowing and their hairs flying and maybe they're walking a dog. You know like "La la la." I would say Lenea is the oldest looking girl in our class. People think she's very good looking and I know what they mean but she isn't my type but I guess

I would probably definitely fool around with her if she wanted to. She's also more serious and not as ditzy as Cindy. Which is why I was surprised to hear her saying stuff about butts but I guess all girls talk about butts basically because guys don't have tits.

Anyway it's around the 6th or 7th or 8th inning between innings so the games been going on for about 95 hours. I haven't said anything in 3 innings and neither has Lenea and Renee hasn't said much except answering questions from Cindy who's like a fountain of talking. Don't get me wrong I still think she's hot and also don't get me wrong the stuff she says isn't that bad sometimes she's even a little funny and she's not totally ditzy as much as I thought but still the more she talks about every 5000 words the amount I think she's hot goes down but I still think she's got a great body. She'd be a great robot. And I could flick the Talk Switch to off. Or Pause. Anyway John comes up in the bleachers between innings his uniform has dirt all over it from this dive he made for a ball he didn't get (he plays 2nd Base) and he's standing in front of us but the 1st thing he says is "Jeremy what's up man?"

"Hey" I say.

"You look cute in that dirty uniform" Renee says.

John pretty much ignores this comment.

"Who's #17 on the other team?" Cindy says.

"Some asshole" John says.

It turns out this guy is talking shit all game which is like shut the fuck up already.

Lenea hands him her Tab and he takes a swig which is kind of surprising because Tab is basically a drink for girls on diets. I suddenly wonder where Randy is because I don't know if

I've ever once in 2 years of High School and 2 years of soccer seen John without seeing Randy but I look down and there he is sitting on the bench picking dirt out of his cleats Randy is actually a pretty good baseball player and has the best batting average on the team.

"I'm on fire today" John says but he's being sarcastic.

"You suck" said Cindy.

"I'm trying to get Jeremy to play ball" John said.

"Oh are you going to play baseball?" Renee said to me.

The whole thing is so weird because it's the middle of the season anyway and you can't just start playing in the middle of the season plus I can't play baseball but I say "I'm thinking about it."

Then John goes back down. Renee Lenea and Cindy look at each other after he goes back down and giggle a little like "Oh John was here". Anyway it's near the end of the game and pretty soon I realize they're all going back in someones car and I don't want them to see me going to the bus which is kind of for losers so I think about going to the bus now but they might see me sitting there so I think about just leaving but it's about 20 miles back to Hutch Falls and there aren't a whole lot of other ways to get there so finally I decide to go get on the bus now and get down low and wait.

"See you guys later" I say and I stand up it's the 9th inning now.

"Bye" says Cindy.

Lenea looks at me but she didn't say anything.

"How are you getting back?" Renee says.

"Um I don't know" I said.

"Come with us" Renee says. "Leneas got a car."

"Oh" I said.

But now I was standing up.

"I'll see you guys in the parking lot" I said.

"OK" said Renee.

They started watching the game again and I went down to the parking lot I diverted towards a few of the other fields and looked at the games going on and stood around where no one knew me and then I went to this place where they have gardens and I walked around because I had a whole inning to kill I wanted to walk towards the parking lot at the same time they were. When I finally went I saw them coming and I walked like I was Mr. Casual and sort of followed them to Leneas car. I said "Hey".

John blew off the team bus to go with us and he sat in front with Lenea and I sat in back with Renee and Cindy I was between the window and Cindy who was blabbing away about butts and other things. She was wearing pretty short shorts and I was wearing normal shorts and our legs were pretty much permanently touching because it was crowded back there but I don't think she even noticed but I noticed because her leg was great.

It was nice of them to give me a ride. I think Renee thinks of me as her Spanish friend so she didn't want to leave me hanging there. But it was weird being with Lenea and Cindy who don't know me at all and with Cindys leg and mine all over each other without her even noticing probably. John I don't think is serious about this whole baseball thing he would give anyone a ride because he's like that. A solid good guy. Even in the halls he's nice to people saying hi and always answering people who say hi to him and everything. He's basically The Great Gatsby. "He smiled understandingly - much more than understandingly. It was one of those rare smiles with a quality of eternal reassurance in it, that you may come across four or five times in a life. It faced - or seemed to face - the whole external world for an instant, and then concentrated on you with an irresistible prejudice in your favor. It understood you just so far as you wanted to be understood, believed in you as you would like to believe in yourself and assured you that it had precisely the impression of you that, at your best, you hoped to convey. Precisely at that point it vanished-" Anyway in the car I didn't really say anything and pretty soon we were back at school. John went to the locker room and the girls drove off somewhere and I was just standing around so I went home. If I had my license I'd give them a ride somewhere to say thanks if they needed 1 but fate decreed I can't do that until June 16.

CHAPTER 20

KATHS GRANDMOTHER BITES THE DUST

Kaths Grandmother had a stroke. Basically her brain exploded she was living alone in an apartment in Philadelphia and she was sleeping but it wasn't 1 of those things where you decompose and you start to smell until the neighbors call the police because they smell it in the hall Kaths mother called the building superintendent when she didn't answer the phone and he went up to the apartment and found her dead in there.

Gillian called and told me and then she said "Kath wants you to be there". We hadn't been out in a couple weeks me with them I mean. I hadn't been out on the balcony either basically we were smiling fake smiles in the hall but it was practically like before we were friends Douglas was the only 1 where we still stopped and talked a lot Caroline wasn't much of a stopper and talker anyway and Kath I didn't run into a lot because she was sick and we had different schedules. Gillian

I think was ignoring me or trying not to be there if I was anywhere. There was just this very big tension between me and
everybody it was like some whole waterfall had started and
we were just stuck in it. Meanwhile I was talking sometimes
in the hall to Renee and John McKnight and Lenea and Cindy
if they were with Renee and sometimes when I'm talking I
see Gillian or Douglas or Caroline go by and I know they see
me and they're probably like "Why are you talking to them?"
except with Caroline it's a little different because she's <u>so</u>
mellow about stuff and doesn't really care what you do and
when she goes by sometimes she says <u>"Hi there"</u>.

Anyway the funeral's on Thursday so for starters I'm missing school in 1 of those "Nobody's going to complain about
you missing school" situations. My Mom drops me off at the
funeral home which is in Chastleton nearby. I have 4 Grand-
parents and 1 died before I was born and 1 died when I was
really young and I didn't go to the funeral which was in Cali-
fornia and 2 didn't die so I've never really been to a funeral
before. I'm wearing a blue Mo Levitskys shirt and a tie and
when I get to the funeral I see everyone but Kath standing out
front Caroline in an even for her pretty gutsy move is wearing
a very short black leather mini-skirt that shows off all her legs
and a black part see through dracula type top and puffing
away but nobody seems to notice (everything's kind of different at funerals like you can do anything). Anyway I go up and
we all hug even me and Douglas and Gillian's crying a little
in that way where you cry a little and stop then cry a little more then stop and she says Kath's really upset and
freaked out and won't talk to her and Gillian seems really

messed up and Douglas looks stupid in a suit I can't explain it it fits and everything but it just looks like he is 1 person who shouldn't be wearing it.

We go inside and there's a service. People talk about Kaths Grandmother and say they loved her so much and what she did in her life which was basically she grew up in this little town in Wisconsin and she left. I could see the side of Kaths face up in the front row. Then we went out to the cemetary where I stood next to Gillian while they lowered her into the ground. It wasn't that sad because she was so old and everything.

When we were leaving the cemetary Douglas and me were walking and he said "I think I'll get cremated".

"Why?" I said.

"I'm not rotting down there with bugs eating my eyes."

"Very nice" I said.

Anyway here's the main thing. We go back to Kaths house for the post-funeral party her house is packed and there's a lot of food which is good because I didn't have breakfast and it turns out funerals make me hungry. So we get there and I'm in the food line surrounded by other people and I don't see anyone anywhere so I get my food and I walk around and finally I see Gillian and Douglas and Caroline standing together in the den I'm sort of 1/2-acting like I don't see them but it just feels weird and I'm about to just go over when I suddenly turn around and head towards the living room and in the hall I run right into Kath.

"Oh Jeremy" she says and hugs me. I hug her back and she starts crying a little but not totally. Then she stops hugging me.

"Hey" I say.

"Thank you for coming" she says.

"Yeah" I said.

She was wearing this blue dress and as you know she's pretty hefty but her cheeks were messed up from where she was crying and her make-up was going all over the place and she actually looks kind of pretty.

"It's good to have your friends around at times like this" I say.

"So we're still friends?" she says and she smiled but her face was kind of sarcastic but not in a mean way.

"Yeah" I say.

"OK" she says.

"The funeral was um" and I don't know what to say.

"Grandma would of liked it" Kath said.

I don't know about that because who likes a funeral when it's theirs.

"How's your Mom?"

It was her Moms Mom who died.

"OK I think she's in shock."

We stood around for a little while. We talked about death.

"It's so strange that she's never coming back. And I don't know where she is" Kath said.

"It's really weird" I said.

"And she died all alone" Kath said.

"That sucks" I said.

"It's so sad."

She shook her head a lot. Eventually I finished my food and I wanted some more and Kath knew I wanted more and she gave me another hug of the "I'm going to the den to talk to everybody else now" variety and she said "You should come out on the balcony."

"Yeah" I said.

I guess I should of said hi to everyone but I didn't. I left soon. Mom picked me up and asked me all about the funeral and everything but I was like "uh-huh" so she'd leave me alone because you want to be left alone after funerals and I was thinking in the car (cars really make me think) about going to a baseball game and getting there late after it's over and everyone's gone except John and Randy are out on the field with about 5 players from Helgrove facing them and John and Randy are like fuck you to them and the 5 guys are trying to start a fight and talking about their mothers and calling them pussys. 2 of the Helgrove guys are huge and when I see what's happening I go up from behind and stand next to John and Randy.

"What's up guys?" I say to John and Randy.

"Hey man" they say.

"Looks like the odds are changing" I say.

The 5 guys don't look so confident anymore but they still outnumber us 5-3 and then the biggest 1 says "Who the fuck are you? You want to get your ass kicked too?"

"I don't see that happening" I say.

"Oh really" this guy says.

"Why don't we settle this just you and me" I say.

He doesn't look so sure.

"What you can only fight when you outnumber people?"

So he comes at me but before he gets there I throw a punch and break his nose. He throws a punch that would kill me if it hit me but I duck and punch him in the ribs and he spins around a little from the force of the blow and I grab him and spin him back and pull his head down and my knee up so I knee him in the chin and he goes down and that's that.

"Anybody else want to have some fun?" I say.

Then I start thinking about flying in a helicopter that's screaming through the sky and jumping out with a parachute and then running through the woods but then slowing down and walking slowly. It's hot. Nightfall is approaching. I have a compass and also I hear sounds and I make my way through trees and bushes and grass and wild birds as it gets darker and creepier I can see huge trees and big flowing rivers everywhere. There are big lions and tigers and bears all over the place. The jungle makes a man desperate. Finally I see the glow of fire. In the distance as I approach I hear John go "Noooooooooooo". He sounds scared. Then as I get really close I hear Cindy going "Let me go you fuckers you suck". Finally I look through the trees and leafs and there's a big circle with tribesmen all around and in the middle tied to a stake is John and Randy and Lenea and Cindy and Renee each 1's on their own stake and they look really terrified and unhappy. Nobody's hurt yet or anything but their clothes are ripped and there's wood and stuff around them so you can tell they're going to set them on fire and then burn them to death. The tribesmen are the Galagangas sworn enemies of the Ife who hate each other because the Galagangas are vicious and also hostile and kill and eat human beings and the Ife are more civilized and eat the Banana Maloosa. Also many years ago a Galaganga Prince killed a Ife elder for nothing and the Ife didn't kill anybody back because they're so peaceful but hated the Galagangas ever since who are also always trying to steal their land. The Galagangas are everywhere and they're wearing those tribal clothes made out of leafs and no shirts and big necklaces and earrings and chanting "Oooaaa Ya Ya Ya" and they're thirsty for blood and banging their drums so loud you can't hear. I look at Lenea who's closing her eyes and looks like she's giving up and Cindy who's still arguing with everybody about everything Randy looks pissed and John was struggling and trying to get out of his ropes. Renee is looking all around and kind of whimpering "Help!" I don't want to end up burning at the stake either but what the hell? I suddenly yell as loudly as I can "Oooooooaaaaaaaa" and then I just walk into the circle in the middle of everything. For a second the Galagangas are like "what the fuck" but then 3 of them rush me I take out my flashlight and shine it in their faces. They stop because only Gods can make light. Everything is quiet then a couple other Galagangas start talking to each other in Galaganga and you can tell they're not psyched-out anymore so when they come towards me I pull up my machine gun and mow them down. Now all the Galaganga are cowering in fear. I take out my knife and cut the ropes and John and Randy and Renee and Lenea and Cindy fall to the ground. I point towards the woods and we all go out we're running like crazy for 10 or 15 minutes when at the last second this huge lion roars and comes flying in the air out of the woods. Its roar is louder than anything you ever heard and it lands right on Randy and starts ripping his face off. I'm right there and I kick the lion in the face but that just distracts him he roars again and comes at me but instead of backing up I pull out my knife again and plunge it into the lions eye. Because the lion is coming towards me with momentum the knife goes all the way in into his brain. The lion screams and then totally freaks out clawing at everything and roaring with saliva on its teeth it jumps on me and we wrestle and it sinks its teeth into my shoulder but I flip it and plunge the knife into its neck and now its dead even though I have to hold it down while it shakes for a minute while its in its death agony. I say "lets go" and we take off again soon we hear a chant of "Ooma chaka ooma chaka" and we start running even faster towards where the helicopter is meeting us. It does and we take off just as the Galaganga are throwing spears and arrows and burning spears at us but we just make it. We're all pretty freaked out even John and Randy who are like "thanks man". "No problem" I said. The girls are comforting each other and then they each kiss me and each other and say thanks and then they go in the back of the helicopter and just gossip and relax.

After we finally got home from the funeral I went to the kitchen for a drink and my Mom was there then my Dad came in then Beth and Claire came in a second later. It was like a family reunion. I said "does anybody want any?" referring to the orange juice in my hand. Nobody did except Claire. My Dad put his hand on my shoulder and said "Death is a part of life Jeremiah".

"I know" I said.

"Um-hmm" he said.

"She was old" I said.

Then I went upstairs.

CHAPTER 21

THE KNICKS GAME

April 23 is a day which will live in infamy. That is the day I got my 1st F. Of course on a Trig quiz. I'm sure it's the 1st F anyone in my family ever got for the last 50 generations. The day I got it I went to talk to Mr. Rasfenjohn who I hadn't really talked to since 1st Semester he said "Math isn't important for you. But passing math is important". Kind of a VTS. Anyway I had a mandatory meeting with my academic counselor who said this could serve as a wake-up call for me and when my Dad found out he was so mad he didn't even really get mad so now I have a tutor who happens to be Mr. Math and he promised I'll pass the final if I do what he says. Also he does explain things in a way I can comprehend sometimes. If I had him instead of Mrs. Lippner I'd probably be passing already. Other than that nothing much happened between Kaths Grandmothers funeral and what I'm about to tell you about next. But it was a pretty crappy couple weeks even though I used to be kind of a loner now I was sort of used to not being 1 and having stuff to do on the weekends and going back sucked. It was like nostalgia or deja voo. But also like I said <u>maybe</u> having millions of friends isn't the most important thing maybe the most important thing is how you feel about yourself and who you are. (This is what Gillian thinks and I think she's right).

Then 1 day here's what happened:

I was stopping and "chatting" with Renee about every 2 days in the hall sometimes we were like "Hey" "Hi Jeremy how're you?" "Fine" and sometimes we talked about anything and also with Cindy and or Lenea and or John McKnight and or Randy. When they were all there or just 3 of them sometimes I'd just walk by and they were so into their conversations and everything they didn't see me but other times Renee would go "Jeremy" or John McKnight would say "Hey Man" and I'd stop and stand there. Anyway I'm talking to Renee and Lenea Lenea by the way when she sees me always says "Hiiiii Jeremy" in this voice like she's goofing around or she's singing or something I'm not sure what she's doing but it's sort of a joke and I always smile like "Ho Ho Ho". So we're standing there and I am making 1 of the superhuman efforts of all time not to look at Renees Tits then which is especially hard today because she's got on a tight very green Polo Shirt that is basically glued to her Tits and every time she turns to look at Lenea I look down and back up so fast my neck gets whiplash and I'm sure any second she's going to go "Jeremy stop staring at my Tits"! I swear I try not to but it's like my eyes aren't responding to the brain commands coming from my head. If you know what I mean. Anyway Renee's saying how psyched she is school's almost over because there's only a month left and she's going to Japan for 3 weeks to see her Japanese friends there like "Kioto" but her dad can't leave work for as long as she wants to go and blah blah blah and Lenea keeps playing with her hair with her hand like she's nervous or something which is funny because I think of her as Miss Very In Control (she's like she's from England or something sometimes) but she's not saying anything and then I hear her go "Jooooooohn" and up comes John McKnight and he's like "Hi girls" (which is pretty smooth) and then he sees me and he goes "What's up J?" So I realize I'm J and I say "Hey."

"Do you guys know Bobby Gurin's in jail?" he said.

"What?" Lenea said.

Renee said "Oh please. He's in jail?"

Bobby Gurin's a senior who's very involved in student union and the school and things like that and you'd never in a billion years expect him to be in jail versus some other people you could sort of expect it.

"He got busted with a prostitute."

"John" said Lenea.

"I'm serious man he called a prostitute in New York and she came to his house and he got busted."

"When?" said Renee.

"Last night."

"He had a prostitute in his house?"

"Yup."

"Really?"

"I'm telling you the cops came and busted him."

"How did they know?" Renee said.

"I don't know."

Then I said "his new platform can be Free Prostitutes For Everyone In The Student Union. And no Police Harassment."

I started trying to figure out if the 1st part of what I said made any sense with the 2nd part but then everyone laughed so I figured it did we had to go to class and John McKnight said to me "Hey man we're watching the Knicks tonight at my place you should come by."

"OK" I said.

Everyone walked away and Renee said "See you tonight" and I got this weird like mini-explosion somewhere and I'd like to say my foot or my head but lets face it it was probably in my heart I don't know why I got it exactly because I've been in love with Renee for a long time but it was like maybe we were going to be friends and that made it worse or like 2 things going closer so they're getting further apart at the same time (like magnets or something else in physics). I didn't know where John McKnight lived.

PART II

Beth dropped me off in front of Johns. I found out where it was. She was impressed because she was like "Have fun" but with a "Whooo hooo" in her voice it wasn't mean though.

John is pretty loaded his house is in 3 Hills which is a fancy part of Hutch Falls with 3 Hills and he's on the 1 in back. His house has a metal lamp in their front yard. I changed into clean blue jeans and I show up and John lets me in and we go into the den where everybody is already there watching the game which hasn't started yet. There were a lot of vases around and things like that that my parents weren't into. As for clothing it was Thursday and John and Randy were wearing T-shirts but the girls were wearing different clothes since school Renee and Cindy were in dresses 1 with flowers and 1 plain and Lenea was wearing these skin-color pants and a vest that matches it over a white shirt that wasn't a T-shirt and she looked like somebodys Mom but hot. John said drinks and stuff were in the kitchen and I went and got orange juice and I came back to watch the game then Reggie Carter goes in in the 2nd Quarter and I say "Carter's underrated."

"You think?" said John.

"Carter sucks" said Randy.

"He just doesn't get any time" I said.

"He makes some decent passes" John said.

"He can't shoot worth shit" Randy said.

"Which 1?" Renee said.

I pointed to Carter.

"Isn't he sort of old" she said.

Just then Carter missed an easy jumper but just barely and Randy goes "See?"

I was bummed.

"He usually hits that" I said.

But he didn't even touch the ball again and then he came out.

"John order a pizza" Cindy commanded.

We talked about what to get on it and then John called and then he went into the kitchen and Lenea followed him. When the pizza came we ate it. Lenea gave her crust to John twice she just put it on his plate without even asking if he wanted it.

At 1 time cheese was dripping down from Renees lips which was very sexy I thought about Gillians lips which as you know from before are really big and cheese dripping down from them but it wasn't sexy like with Renee it was just cheesy.

Even all through the 2nd 1/2 the girls didn't complain about watching the game the way Beth and Mom would if we ever even got near a channel where there was a basketball game on not that my Dad would ever watch basketball. Randy talked like after Richardson sunk a shot he'd say "Did you see that shot?" and other obvious stuff. I always saw him like Johns sidekick like Robin or Tonto but being there it seemed more like he was his robot. We were in the kitchen at 1 point getting more drinks just the 2 of us and he said "You want ice?" so he was nice and everything but he stood like a robot and I was like "Somebody should inject a personality into you." I could tell the girls all thought the same thing if they thought about it.

Cindy left to do a Chem assignment and Lenea sat next to John on the couch during the 4th Quarter I was on the floor next to a chair with Renee in it. John looked over at Renee sometimes Lenea leaned over and said things in Johns ear I was too close and too under Renee to look at her but I could feel her in a mysterious way there in the chair watching. Lenea at 1 point said "Jeremy are there any Tabs left?" because I was just in the kitchen and I said "Yeah" and she smiled at me in that "so maybe you'd like to get me 1" way. I was definitely in a Catch-22. This famous saying comes from Joseph Hellers famous book Catch-22 which is often recommended. If you read it you should know Catch-22 is a very bulky book and 1 thing you can do is rip it up as you go so if you read say 20 pages you can rip them off and then if you read the next 20 pages rip them off and as you go the book gets smaller and smaller then you can just put all the parts back together with a rubber band again after you finish (which I almost am). A Catch-22 is when it sucks if you do it this way and it sucks if you do it the other way.

    Yossarian looked at him soberly and tried another approach. "Is Orr crazy?"

    "He sure is," Doc Daneeka said.

    "Can you ground him?"

    "I sure can. But first he has to ask me to. That's part of the rule."

    "Then why doesn't he ask you to?"

    "Because he's crazy," Doc Daneeka said. "He has to be crazy to keep flying combat missions after all the close calls he's had. Sure, I can ground Orr. But first he has to ask me to."

    "That's all he has to do to be grounded?"

    "That's all. Let him ask me."

    "And then you can ground him?" Yossarian asked.

    "No. Then I can't ground him."

    "You mean there's a catch?"

    "Sure there's a catch," Doc Daneeka replied. "Catch-22. Anyone who wants to get out of combat duty isn't really crazy."

This reminds me of Who's On 1st by Laurel and Hardy if you ever saw it. Anyway if I didn't get her a Tab I was trying to play it cool and not be her slave but she wouldn't think I was very nice to her. If I got her a Tab she'd think I was nice and cool but also think I was her slave and I'd do anything for her and maybe had no confidence or manhood. So I was in a Catch-22.

Mom kind of reminds me of Capt. Yossarian by the way.

Anyway I groaned like getting the Tab was a huge deal but then I did it as a favor and when I came back with it and a glass of ice Lenea said "thanks hon".

Nothing else much happened. When I went home Beth said "How was it?" "Cool" I said. "What did you do?" "We watched the game." I went up to my room I thought about how hot and sexy Renee and Lenea and Cindy were and all the Tits in the room. I didn't talk a lot. I made no - 0 - good jokes. I wondered if they'd invite me to the next game but I didn't care that much I'd go but it wasn't a matter of life or death or anything.

CHAPTER 22

THE CONVERTIBLE

If somebody like God had come up to me on the 1st day of school and said "Jeremiah Reskin by the end of the year you will be driving in a car alone with Renee Shopmaker - And she will be wearing her Kimono" I would not of believed him and I would of been right about the Kimono part but as for the other part . . .

It's weird how you can talk to somebody every single day and then not at all. For example Gillian. I didn't even see her anymore except sometimes when the halls were crowded I'd coincidentally see the side of her hair going by a few people away like curls going by. Or sometimes I'd see her whole face coming at me but for 1 millisecond. Sometimes when the phone rang I thought it was her.

Versus Kath and Douglas and Caroline who I still say "hi" to and Douglas and me walk home at the same time sometimes and we see each other and sometimes we go up Brian

Hill together and talk about stuff like how Kath is dealing with her Grandmother being dead and the summer. We never talk about him and Caroline and what is going on there which I think is nothing. Once I saw Caroline outside school standing around and smoking and I talked to her for a couple minutes. Her and Richie broke up but they were still seeing each other and she didn't seem into Douglas she said she was taking time off from guys. I thought that was a good idea just to sort of get her head together. And learn to be alone.

Anyway Renee and John and everybody was like "come talk to us when we're talking" and they start almost expecting me to be there talking to them if I'm there it's like I must stop. Nobody says "Hey Jeremy come here" I just come over. So 1 day I went with them to another boring baseball game but I wasn't at anyones house again after Johns before 1 time when I was talking to Renee in Spanish and we were doing a dialogue drill with the verb "Querer"[1] and she said "Jeremy tu quieres ir con me nueva york?"[2] So of course I say "Si yo quiero ir con tu nueva york".[3] And then Renee says "Sabado?"[4] and now I'm like Huh? because we're just saying stuff to use the verb Querer so she's getting pretty specific with Sabado. Like if she said "Do you want to go to Disneyland?" and I said "Yes" and she said "How about Thursday at 2:18 P.M." (which would be fine by the way if we were doing a dialogue drill with Hours and Minutes but we're not). So I say "Si" and she

1. To want
2. Jeremy do you want to go with me to New York
3. which basically means yes
4. which I can never remember if it's Saturday or Sunday but I know it's 1 of the 2. By the way it's Saturday.

says "Great. Yo tengo - yo tengo - I have to" and just then Mr. Eller says "Termine Dialogue."

Now this is on Wednesday and I still think Renee's just kidding not joking but just she was doing Spanish but I'm not positive and there's this voice in me that keeps going "No she really wants to go to New York with you" but she doesn't say anything again and I'm just playing it cool like "I'm not an idiot" so if she thinks we're going I can be like "Yeah I know we're going" and if she never brings it up again for the rest of our lifes I can be like "I never thought you were going to bring it up again."

Then on Friday she brings it up again. It's Friday and we're standing with everybody and Lenea says something about a classical music concert (SNORE) she's going to with her parents on Saturday and Renee says "Jeremy's going to New York with me." I just sort of smile and nod my head like "Yup. I knew that all along."

Then at the end of Friday she says to me "I'll pick you up at 9:30 I know it's crazy early but I have to go see my Uncle at 1:00 and I have a lot of errands to do 1st."

"OK" I say.

I get up at 8:30 Saturday morning and shower and put on Old Spice and for clothing I put on a long sleeve button down dark blue shirt of my Dads I got out of his closet the night before and rolled the sleeves up so it was like a short sleeve shirt which John does sometimes but he tucks it in and I had it tucked out. I'm standing in the living room looking out the window when my Mom comes downstairs wearing her robe that she lounges around in on Saturday mornings when I'm not up and says "what are you doing up so early?"

My Mom in her robe looks like Dawn Of The Dead. 1st of all her hair is flying all over and on top of her face and she just looks like she's dead.

"Nothing" I said. "I might be going into the city later."

Anyway she never came I waited until about 10:30 and I gave up but I hung around in case she showed up late. I realized it was just a Spanish dialogue thing after all and then when she said to everybody we were going she was making a follow-up joke on that so when I saw them Monday I'd just be like "Hey" and they'd never know I didn't know. The next morning I'm sound asleep like a baby in my bed when my Mom knocks on the door and I hear "Your friend Renee's here." OK if you take the fastest thing you ever saw (for example Beth when the phone rings) and multiply it by 10,000 that's how fast I got dressed I didn't even know what was going on I was just like shirt pants socks run downstairs act like you were already ready you just needed a second to get down.

"Hi" said Renee she was smiling and standing there in a red sweater with a missing V and blue jeans and her face was beautiful underneath her hair which looked short today because it was tied up in back. My Mom was smiling and I said "Later" and we went outside where in front of the house was an old dark red Mustang Convertible I went around the other side and got in.

"Hey" I said.

"Good morning Jeremy Reskin (she called me this sometimes)."

She smiled and we took off.

"Sweet wheels" I said.

"It's my Dads" she said.

I didn't say anything about the whole Sabado Domingo thing which was probably my fuck-up anyway.

We drove through Hutch Falls and then onto the NJ Turnpike the wind was blowing our hair all over the place and the car was so old and classic I felt like I was in a commercial or an old movie about driving. Renee had the radio on WXUF which is totally black people music believe me I wasn't going to say "Hey lets put on MRQ" but this stuff was actually pretty good for driving Renee was driving pretty straight but once in a while if the music got super funky she started dancing a little with her shoulders and it was pretty sexy and before you knew it the car was going into other lanes and I was like "We're going to die". I saw her Tits in profile by the way and then there were no sleeves on her shirt and I could see in her arm hole where there was the strap of her bra which was black and her Tits didn't move much and she had black sunglasses on and it felt like being in a movie with a very very very sexy movie star.

It takes an hour and 18 minutes to drive to NY according to my Dad. I've driven a few times with my Dad and once with Douglas but I had no idea how to get there because you don't really get your sense of direction unless you're driving and I still don't have my fucking license which sucks but I'll get it almost as soon as the summer starts. Anyway once we were there I recognized things and when Renee said "Which way is uptown?" I said "That way" and even though I was wrong I knew where I was going. People in New York look at you when you're in a convertible or maybe when you're with Renee 1 guy shouted when he was crossing the street and we were at a red light "Get it while you can kid" which I made a face at Renee like "What an idiot" but because he thought I was getting some from Renee I was kind of like "alright". In fact Renee was stopping at stores and picking stuff up for her Mother and dropping stuff off for her Mother and I kept waiting in the car so we didn't get towed but I wanted to go in the stores and have more people admiring me there obviously with her. Well we got a parking place near BloomingDales which is a very famous store in New York and so I went in with her and it was really crowded and nobody even saw us but then we went to the 3rd Floor because we were shopping here for a bathing suit and up there in the womens bathing suit dept. I was the only guy anywhere and the women who were all older who worked there did look at us funny and had this sort of "Aren't they cute" attitude and I definitely didn't say anything like "No I've never actually touched or seen any of those Tits."

So Renee keeps looking at these bathing suits and she says "Do you like bikinis or 1 pieces?"

"Um it depends on what you want" I say "I mean I like bikinis but 1 pieces are cool too."

My interpretation of her question is it's like "Do you like Ice Cream or Milk Shakes?"

If everybody told the truth I would say: "I like 1 pieces because you get to see more of what you don't see and then you can imagine the persons overall Tits but I guess I'd have to go with the bikini if God made me choose 1 because of overall being closer to no bikini on at all and seeing all the cleavage and the whole stomach and everything under the Tits and now you can see everything almost just like what it's really like" and even though Renee was standing right there next to me I started picturing her 1st in the really light red 1 piece she was looking at a second before that was so small on its own I didn't even see how she'd stretch it over her big Tits and her body and then in the purple bikini she was holding now that was purple on the outside but white inside and the inside part was soft.

"Hmm" Renee said.

Then she goes into the dressing room with the purple 1 and I'm like "Uh-Oh" for some reason her being naked in the dressing room there in the store with the carpet and everything seemed even better than seeing her in it on the beach with sand and the sun and water and everything. Probably because I was in the store and I wasn't on the beach.

And then I heard some footsteps and she came out of the dressing room and she was wearing nothing but the purple bikini and it was the 1st time I'd really seen actual parts of her. And I felt myself think "Oh Man" and before I could do anything she turned around really fast and went back in the dressing room I was like "Uhhhhhhhh" like I was dying and a minute later she came back out totally dressed and she said "Let's go." I said "OK" but she seemed upset and I said "What's wrong?" "Nothing" she said. I acted like everything was totally cool then she said "I don't know they're so, big." I said "Errunnnuhhh." Then I woke up. Except I didn't. Because I wasn't sleeping. This was all happening. I looked around a little like there was stuff to look at. Then I said "I don't think people always think the things people think they think." "What do you mean?" she said. "I don't know." When we were walking out I was checking out bikinis like it would give her the bright idea of trying on some more but that didn't happen.

We went to her Uncle Arthurs apartment she kept saying he was really cool but with a name like Uncle Arthur I pictured some total nerd in glasses. When we got there he did have glasses but he wasn't a nerd he was about 40 and he wore a kind of bright black Sport Jacket with a shirt and no tie and black shoes that were shiny and he looked weird but in an OK cool way and his apartment was basically the coolest place I've ever been there were 2 floors but just 1 big room with a very very very high ceiling (I didn't know they made ceilings that high) that went all the way to the top and was the ceiling of the 2nd floor too. There were sculptures all over and they were a lot of wood African guys with their wood dicks sticking out and African women with their Tits showing but that's just how they live in Africa. Renee gave Uncle Arthur a big hug and kiss and said "Hi Uncle Arthur" then she said "this is my friend Jeremy." "Hi Jeremy" he said. "Hey" I said. "Call me Arthur" he said. "OK" I said.

He started showing me around and he said "Jeremy are you familiar with African Tribal Art?" "Uncle Arthur is an art dealer" Renee said. "Yeah" I said. "Do you know about the Banana Maloosa?"

"No" said Arthur.

"It's an African Tribal dish. A delicacy."

"Hmm" said Uncle Arthur. "Where did you have that?"

"I made it".

"You made it?" said Uncle Arthur. "That's very impressive how was it?"

"Pretty bad."

We all laughed.

We all sat down on big white couches.

"How's school Babe?" Arthur said to Renee.

"Oh it's the same" she said.

"Do you have a boyfriend?"

I don't know how he knew I wasn't her boyfriend.

"No" said Renee "but there's this guy he goes to another school I think he's cute but we've only talked a few times."

I was like Wo I didn't know about that even though I'd so given up and never had any chance in the 1st place with Renee but still I wanted to run over and jump through the big windows and crash through the glass and before I splattered on the ground outside yell "Reneeeeee!" I had no idea who this guy from the other school was.

"I know the boys are standing in line for you sweetheart but take your time and pick the right 1."

"I know" she said.

"What about you Jeremy?" Uncle Arthur said to me.

"Schools OK" I said "I'm ready for summer though."

"I'll bet you are" said Arthur who was laughing about it. "What are your plans?"

"My Dad has this friend who's a partner at a law firm where they might need a messenger hopefully I'll do that. We usually go on a family trip too but I'm not sure I'm going this year."

"The law firm you'll be working at is in NY?"

"Yeah I'll take the train with my Dad in the morning."

"Let me know if you do that I'll take you to lunch. We'll give you a little break from carrying packages."

"OK" I said.

Renee smiled at me I'm not sure why but I think because Uncle Arthur was going to take me to lunch.

Then Uncle Arthur reached down to the coffee table opened a little box and took out a joint! I was like 'Wo! Holy shit!' I looked at Renee who didn't look surprised and then Uncle Arthur lit it and took a puff then he handed it to Renee WHO TOOK IT AND TOOK A PUFF. I really really didn't know Renee smoked pot I thought she was very uptight about drugs and stuff probably I didn't think John or any of them were into drugs but here was Renee Shopmaker puffing away AND WITH HER Uncle and she handed me the joint AND I took a puff. I didn't even stop to think about it 1st I just did it and then I'd done it.

Thank God for watching those other guys smoke Pot enough that I know how to do it and not take a huge puff so I cough my guts out.

Now there's 1 other thing about Uncle Arthur which is he's a flaming Faggot but even though I thought this he was Renees uncle and it was sort of like who cares?

We hung out and smoked more and then we left. I was just like 'man this is so fucking weird' but then I wasn't anymore and I was just happy to be with Renee and hungry.

Here's what it's like when I'm High: like everything is totally different. And I, Jeremiah Reskin am totally different. It's pretty cool. I'm also paranoid like if I see a dog walking I think it's a giant wolf and I think everything's funny like just me being me makes me laugh and anything anyone says is funny even if it's not funny and I'm starving for pizza or chips or huge pieces of cardboard if that's all there is. And Renees Tits are like a holy altar I worship and I don't even know if she's busting me or not but sometimes she giggles for no reason and I wonder if it's why she's giggling but a lot of times you just giggle for no reason. Anyway I don't remember what but we eat and we walk around NY and we drink coffee which I drink black and Renee drinks with cream and sugar and now we're not that High anymore. Then we drive home in the car Renee says "Lenea needs a date for The Prom."

Prom is only for Seniors and Juniors but knowing these guys they just go anyway. They have Senior and Junior friends.

"Yeah?" I say.

"Uh-huh John's taking me and she doesn't want to go with Randy Dan Schmit asked her but she said she already has a date because she doesn't know him at all."

I said "it's good to go with someone you know."

"Who's Dan Schmit?" I said.

"He's that Junior with the thing. You know that saxophone."

"Oh" I said.

"Oh why don't you ask her?" Renee said.

"Um I don't know."

"I think she'd go with you."

"Yeah?"

"Uh-huh she likes you. You know as a friend she thinks you're cute too it's not that but she's just so into John."

"That must be weird with him taking you and all."

"Oh you don't even know I don't know what to do about it. I think I should of said "No" to John."

"Why? I mean you have to go to Prom."

"I know. But I don't like John like that I should of made him take Lenea."

"If he's not into Lenea he's not into her."

"I agree with you."

We just drove for a second. Here's what I have to say about the NJ Turnpike. We live in a great country called America and our highways and Turnpikes connect 1 part of this great land to all the others.

"So you should ask her" Renee said.

"Hmm" I said.

"She'd definitely say yes."

"Hmmm" I said.

CHAPTER 23

PROM

Rule #1: get your Drivers License before Prom. I've got my Permit but what am I going to do pick her up with my Dad in the back seat? But Randy to the rescue we've colonized this area between the soccer field and the parking lot where the bike racks are and we sit there on the racks and the guys hang out sometimes and we're talking about where we're taking our dates for dinner and what it's going to cost and everything and Randy goes "I'm drinking beers at Jeffs" (Jeff is a guy on the baseball team who's having an all night after-Prom party and Randy and John are friends with him from baseball so we're basically invited.) John says "Renee likes wine with dinner if they serve us."

"You get served when you're dressed up" I say.

"Even though they know you're going to Prom?" John says.

"Yeah they take pity on you."

Anyway the point is they both had their Licenses but they

didn't want to drink and drive which is very responsible so Randy goes "Let's get a Limo." John points out that costs a mint and I say we can split it and John says "what'll it do stop everywhere everyones going?" and Randy says "Yeah" so we decided to do it. And we decided to meet at Johns in our Tuxs and all the guys will go together except Cindys date unless he wants in on it and then we'll go get the girls.

Here's the conversation trying to get my Dad to cough up the extra $65:

"Dad we're going to split a Limo to Prom."

"A Limousine isn't that expensive?"

"Kind of but not that much."

"Can't your sister drive you?"

"Are you joking?"

"Why not?"

"Dad."

"How much is it?"

"$65."

"$65?"

My Dad likes to repeat things with a question mark.

"Yeah."

"I'll tell you what I'll pay 1/2."

I was working that summer so I said OK.

I won't bore you to death with all the stuff about deciding where to go and Claire sending me back with my 1st Tux to get a 2nd 1 that looked way better and renting the Limo but we all ended up in a long and dark and black Limo the night of Prom except for Cindy whose date didn't know any of us and picked her up in his car. Lenea when we picked her up

2nd to last looked so beautiful John said "Damn" and Randy said "Yow" even though she was my date and Renee was already in the Limo Lenea looked so beautiful I even forgot for a second I wasn't in love with her and that Renee was in the car looking extra-beautiful too. Renee had on a black dress that stopped being a dress far from her neck and so showed a little cleavage and then was more like a skirt lower and ended on top of her knees. Leneas dress was totally different it was white and had flowers on it and straps and even though she looked even more totally old and grown-up then usual suddenly at Prom that seemed great she was totally like a woman and her hair that she always had long and straight was kind of curly I guess from curling it and she got in the Limo and sat down next to me and instead of feeling stupid the way I did in my Tux and the way probably John and Randy did in their Tuxs because they're just Monkey Suits she was like "Hi everybody." No don't worry I'm not going to suddenly fall in love with her in the Limo on the way to Prom but I felt like I could definitely be friends with her.

So we make the rounds of the restaurants. John and Renee are going to Cafe Tres Canards which means "Cafe 3 Ducks" in French it's a very fancy place my parents go on their anniversary behind the mall then me and Lenea get out at Jimmys which is way way way nicer and fancier than it sounds Randy and his date went to the Meadowbrook Grill which I tried to talk him out of because it's overrated and not that good and I've gone there with my parents twice and had steak that was basically a slab of meat.

We had a reservation and when we went to our table pretty

much everyone in the universe was looking at us partly because I'm in a fucking Tuxedo but partly also I think because Lenea is about the most beautiful woman in the place.

We each order an appetizer and a salad and soup and a main course. I order Filet Mignon which is my favorite steak and if I'm with my family I only get it if it's a special occasion like my Birthday or something because it's so expensive. I also order Pumpkin Soup and house salad and for my appetizer Greco Chicken Appetizer. Lenea gets fish causing me to say "Fish?" and her to say "I like fish. Don't you like fish?"

"Not really" I say.

Then she gets Vichiswaz which is potato soup and also house salad and these little mushroom hats basically filled with some vegetables and stuff inside.

At 1st we were like 'what do we talk about now'? because we were never really alone before now for more than about a minute but then she said "What are you doing this summer" and I told her about my job (messenger) and she told me more about this bicycle trip she was going on in France. It turned out she's really into travel and foreign cultures and seeing the world. Lenea thinks we have to see how other people live to understand them and ourselves. Which I think too it's sort of like with the Ife and other tribes and how they have puberty festivals and how if you know that then you know we don't have puberty festivals. Which I told her. Except I said "Festivals for passing into manhood". And she said "Jeremy you're really smart."

Then we talked about all the stuff like being Juniors next year and college and I thought about saying I wasn't going to college but I didn't want to give her the wrong impression so

I didn't say anything and besides maybe I was going to college who knows. (By the way I passed Math so I can be a Junior. On the final I got a D+/C− which Mr. Math when he found out gave me a thumbs up which made us both laugh because we both knew it really sucked but at least I passed).

Over steak and fish Lenea told me how she wanted to be a lawyer specializing in human rights and international refugees it was a whole side of her I didn't know and had never seen before. I said I have no idea what I want to be and she said what do you like to do and I thought for a second and said soccer and she said well what classes and I said No classes and she said None and I said I liked Mr. Rasfenjohn 1st Semester. And she said you could be a writer. And I said "Uhhuh."

I had chocolate cake with rasberry topping all over it and Lenea had fruit tart for dessert. We both had cafe (which is pretty much coffee) which was actually pretty good.

I paid the check and then I asked the Maitre D if I could use the phone and I called the guy at the Limo place. Everyone had to be done by 8:15 and even though it was exactly 8:15 it turned out we were the last ones done and John and Renee had already gone to Prom and when he picked us up Randy and his date were in the Limo. His date was named Wendy. She was from Florida and I don't know what the hell she was doing in Hutch Falls to go to Prom with Randy I think they knew each others families and saw each other sometimes during the summer and she flew here to go to Prom with him. Or maybe they were cousins or something. But anyway she was tall and kind of big but not bad big more like good big she had very blond hair and a white red face probably from living in Florida all the time and she was 1 of those sort of super-American style girls. She was pretty cute actually. Like you'd want to play Frisbee with her and have sex with her at the same time. She was wearing this red dress with no sleeves and what would be cleavage if she had any. We didn't really talk in the Limo and I didn't know if she knew Randy was kind of a dope or if she was madly in love with him or what but he put his hand on her knee in the Limo and she didn't do anything. (But maybe she was just being nice).

Prom was at the Sheraton Executive Towers in downtown Hutch Falls. Everybody was already there by the time we got there it was very crowded. There weren't any Sophomores there except for us but nobody cared and not everybody knew us anyway so they didn't even necessarily know we were Sophomores. John and Renee were in the Main Ballroom by the wall and drinking Tab and Punch John was wearing a white Tuxedo jacket by the way and standing there with the cup in his hand he looked like James Bond or something.

"What's up?" he said.

He gave me and Randy Hi-5s and I was kind of like that's dumb to do at a fancy occasion like this but Renee wasn't even looking she was looking over at the dance floor like she was daydreaming.

Anyway we were all standing around talking and here's what it was like: like when we stood around talking in the hall except in Tuxedos. Except it was different because I swear those Tuxedos do something to you everything is weird and different. There was a band of older guys and they were playing older stuff like When I Need You and new stuff like Bette Davis Eyes (who my Dad said was quite an actress) and slow songs like Do That To Me 1 More Time that nobody knew I like even though I do and I was for whatever reason more into Renee than ever maybe because it was Prom. It was dark in the Main Ballroom and Randy and his date go to dance and then John and Renee go to dance and Cindy and her date who graduated from Hutch Falls a year ago go outside either to make out or just get some air and then me and Lenea are standing there twiddling our thumbs and she was like "Well?" but there was a fast song on and I can't fast dance so I didn't say anything and I was wishing we could talk some more about our futures and stuff or whatever but dinner was over and we just sort of stood there. Then after about 5 million songs they start playing Sometimes When We Touch and Lenea was like "well?" again but just sort of with her eyes and expression and this 1 was slow and 1 of my favorite songs of all time so this time I just go "Do you want to dance?"

She grabbed my hand and pretty much pulled my arm off pulling me out there and then we're dancing. I guess the truth is I never really danced before and basically here's what you do: turn around. In a circle. That's it. With a beautiful woman all over you. So in particular Leneas Tits were smashed into me even with her dress and my shirt and my Tux jacket bottom line is her Tits were all over me. You can totally feel them and they weren't big but they were there 2 soft parts of her and all I can tell you is if you ever get a chance to dance do it and we were turning around and I think I was sort of naturally pretty good or OK at it because of soccer and just being an athlete and the music was going and I wasn't listening to the words really but I heard that part of Sometimes When We Touch that you might or might not know that goes "At times I think we're drifters still searchin for a friend a brother or a sister but then the passion flares again" and I forgot about Renee for a second and I felt Lenea all over me and I was like are we like a brother or a sister and is the passion flaring again? Then I thought about Renee I looked around but there were a lot of people and she was off dancing with John somewhere and I didn't see her.

We danced some more then we got Cokes. I saw John talking to some Juniors. They were all laughing and having a good time. Me and Lenea were I think closer now and we just stood around then Cindy and her date came over he was this big oaf who played football and he obviously didn't want anything but to fuck her and she didn't know or seem to mind her hair was so curly anyway but I guess she'd curled it because it was even curlier now like just a huge blond thing of curls on her head. It looked good. Her idiot date liked talking about all his football injuries he had when he played football and Cindy and Lenea were like "Ooooh" and I was like Give Me A Fucking Break and why don't you play a skill sport like soccer where people don't kill each other. Then I saw Renee go up to John who was about 35 feet away talking to the Juniors and she put her arm in in kind of a loop in his.

Was Prom fun? I don't know. Cindy got this big smile and was like "So Jeremy do you want to dance?" like it was some big deal or something and so we danced and John and Renee were obviously having a good time except John's always having a good time but Renee isn't and she was smiling and was tonight she danced with John and about 50 other guys who because she was Renee just wanted to dance with her and came up and asked and she said yes and danced 1 dance with them. John didn't care he was dancing with other girls too I don't think he even cared about his thing for Renee he went out at 1 time or another this year with Millicent Burgen and had sex according to him anyway with Andrea Wayne and Alexa Janovich. Randy and his date would show up and talk for a while then disappear then show up again then disappear again they didn't dance or at least I never saw them.

I go outside for some air. It's nice out and I'm thinking. But who's out there but Cindy and her idiot date and I notice her asking me and a few other people if they know anybody who has any cigarettes her idiot date is saying "come on baby we'll take a drive and get some" but she's still looking and she goes inside and comes back still without any. Then he's like "Lets go" and she goes "OK OK lets go" he's been drinking I know because he's got a flask and when Cindy went inside and we were just standing there saying nothing he swigged it a few times and also just the way he is and everything I can tell he's toasted and definitely too wasted to drive. So they start going to the parking lot and I say "hey man I'll drive you" (Yes I don't have my license but I'm a good driver and I'd rather drive without it then let this situation develop). "Huh?" he says. "I'll drive I haven't been drinking or anything." "Hah" he more or less says. We're basically in the middle of the parking lot further from the Prom now. "It's no big deal" I say "I'll take you." This time he just ignores me the thing is he's holding the keys and I'm walking right next to him and I just reach down and grab them I think because he's drunk and everything he doesn't really have the reflexes he would to stop me. Plus he's a dumb lame ass football player. I kind of scoot back a little in case he decides to tackle me. So I take the keys and he's like "Huh?" and I say "Let me drive you it's no big deal" and he looks at me and he's like "I got a idea give me my keys before I kill you." "Look man" I say then he shouts louder "I'm not fucking around doosh bag give me my fucking keys" but I don't. "I'm counting to 3 then you die" he says. I stood there and I wasn't sure what I was going to do then Cindy suddenly says "Pete I don't want to go anymore lets go back inside." "You don't want cigarettes?" he says. "I don't feel like smoking" she says "Lets go inside." "Keys" he said. So I toss him the keys he almost drops them but he catches them. I get way out of his way when he goes by and when I turn around I see that John is walking way in front of them back to the hotel so I guess he was there behind me somewhere. I wait in the parking lot and get some air when they go back in. I just stood there for a while. Football players often are oafs. What a jerk.

So the night was going on. And on. And then it was almost over. Prom and all that it meant was coming and going. I liked the music and a few times I looked in Leneas eyes for a second but she was usually looking away especially near the end she looked depressed maybe because of John or something it wasn't because of me there was nothing there. For me either. Except we were really good friends now.

Most of the Juniors and Seniors had cars but a lot of them had Limos too and when we went out to the parking lot we couldn't even tell which 1 was ours. Everyone was getting in their cars and Limos and laughing and had their arms around each other it was a really special time. None of us had arms around each other except Randy and Wendy. Mr. Football had his hands in his pockets but looked like he wanted to put them somewhere else and Cindy was walking right, right next to him. So we got in the Limo and went off to the Shore which was an hour away.

"I'm tired" said Lenea as she yawned and put her arms up and stretched them.

"You're going all night baby" John said.

Eventually we get to the Shore I've been there before because my parents friends the Hausers have a house there and especially when we were little we used to go there for the weekend. The Hausers kids were older so we had very little in common but I know now their daughter was pretty hot and the truth is I always thought it was boring just going to the beach and having bar-b-q's and stuff and a lot of times you'd be down there at night bar-b-qing and there'd be tons of other people down there with bonfires bar-b-qing too or having clam bakes and laughing their heads off and running in the water at night and basically I just always thought it sucked.

Well when we get to Jeffs house which was pretty nice we went inside. A lot of people changed before they left Prom or in their Limos I guess but we didn't and we were in the house there are a lot of people around but pretty soon most of them go to the beach and most of my friends did too because I was standing talking in the dining room where only 1 or 2 other people were to Lenea and drinking a Coke and Lenea said "Lets go to the beach." "OK" I said. "Lets change" she said. Now I forgot to think about swimming at the after-Prom even though I was thinking about the after-Prom and I knew it was at the shore and I didn't bring a bathing suit so I said "I didn't bring a bathing suit". "We'll find you 1" said Lenea. She was confident. "OK" I said so she starts looking for the stairs upstairs and I just pretty much follow her and we go upstairs and there's nobody up there we go in this 1 room and Lenea starts opening the drawers but there's no bathing suit. "It's a beach house I'm sure there's a bathing suit somewhere" she says so we go in another room and she again looks in the drawers but no bathing suit. Finally we go in the last bedroom which isn't the master bedroom but is probably like a guest bedroom at the end of 1 hall this room is a good setting for a beach house there's a bed and this rug on the floor in front of the bed and there's stuff on the walls like pictures and crafts. She looks in the drawers again and nothing no bathing suit so I say "I don't really want to swim anyway". Which I don't just because I didn't feel like it. "Oh" she said.

Then she said "Here Jeremy can you help me with this?" She turns around and picks her hair up off her back and neck so I could get in and help her unzip her beautiful Prom dress. Her hair remember is very black and long and beautiful like when you picture a beautiful woman you picture this hair if you're thinking about hair. I said "Yeah". So I go over and the zipper is really long all the way down almost to her ass and I unzip it. And then before anything Lenea just slides out of it so it collapses on the floor and she's in nothing but her bra and underwear Lenea as I said before is very foxy and I'm looking at her back which I never really saw before backs are actually really big they're so much of the body and then she walks over to her bag she put on the bed and picks it up and goes into the bathroom which is behind me. She closes the door some but not all the way like she pushed it but not hard I start to say "I'll see you downstairs" but when I'm at around the l in I'll she says "I'll be right out" before I did so I turn around and I'm closer to the bathroom and farther from the bed and I see

inside where the door is open part way and partly I see her
and partly there's a huge mirror in there on the wall and I see
the rest of her suddenly she takes her hand and puts it behind
her and undoes her bra which goes flying off I see the side of
her breasts right there and I look in the mirror and there I see
the rest of them and I don't keep looking in the mirror I kind
of look away near the wall but then I look back and she kind
of moves behind the door where I can't see her or in the mirror except then her leg comes out and her underwear is sliding down then her other leg then I don't know what happened
and a second later she just comes out and she's sort of holding
her bikini top up in front of her to carry it so it's like she's got
her arms in front of her Tits but not definitely on purpose but
you can't cover your whole Tits with your arms and there is a
lot of them in the middle and coming out the side and top and
bottom and everywhere even though they're not huge there's
still a lot of them and she's got blue jeans on I guess with her
bathing suit bottoms on under them and she says "tie this for
me" and she walks 4 or 5 feet to me and I'm pretty sure I
stared for a second but lucky for me she was there in 1 second
and turned back around. "OK" I say. Leneas back is right in
front of me and she just stands there. I don't know what she's
doing thinking about something? Waiting? Adjusting the bikini
top or something? Part of me is super close to just putting my
hand on her back or grabbing her Tits. Then after a while she
pulls the top up and on her Tits in front and reaches around
and hands me the strings and I say "Uh" by accident and she
says "just a regular knot double". So I do that and then she
goes back to the bathroom where her bag still is and puts on a
T-shirt over it and comes back out and puts gym shoes on with

no socks then she says "Are you going to change?" because
I've got jeans and stuff and I say "Yes" and she says "I'll see
you out there" and I change into jeans and a T-shirt and go
down to the beach where guess what we're having a giant
clam bake. I was still stuffed from dinner and I hate clams so
I didn't have any but the girls were feasting away like they
hadn't eaten in 10 years and Randy and John were eating and
some of us had beers. Obviously you're not supposed to drink
at the after-Prom but if there were Chaperones I didn't see
them and they couldn't see anything anyway like if you were
holding a beer or a Coke in your hand or whatever because it
was totally dark out. There were huge shadows everywhere
from the huge bonfire that was already raging when we got
there. It smelled like sand. And clams.

I sat down on the sand with the girls except Randys date
who was with some people we just met and John and Randy
and Cindys date Pete were off playing night frisbee with some
guys. Everybody thought Prom was pretty cool and it was a
beautiful night.

"We're really lucky you know" said Renee.

"I know" said Lenea.

"It's so beautiful and here we are and we've had really good
lifes so far. I just think this is 1 of those nights where you
really appreciate things."

She was sitting there in the sand and we weren't very far
from the fire and her face was sort of 1/2 lit up red by it but
the other 1/2 was totally dark and even though you couldn't
even exactly see her she looked more beautiful than ever. And
here she was talking and I just said "I feel really lucky."

"Why?" said Lenea.

I didn't know what to say so I said "Well it's so beautiful and everything. And we're all here together."

"Oh Jeremy" Renee said.

"That's so sweet" Lenea said and she leaned over and gave me a huge hug.

We talked a lot philosophically that night. Later I was sitting with Lenea and Renee and John and Lenea made the point that it wouldn't be that long before we were at our Senior Prom and at the party afterwards and then going off to start our lifes. John said "starting different lifes" and we were like "Yeah" except for Renee who said "No it's the same life."

And then I don't even know how it happened but I was taking a walk with Renee down the beach a lot of people at the party were walking back and forth so there were people around but especially when we got a little further away there weren't other people. We were just talking about Sophomore Year being over and how weird it was then Renee said "it was weird with John having this thing for me all year."

"Yeah" I said.

"I know all the girls like him and he's a great guy and everything. He's just not my type there's no chemistry between us. You know chemistry is everything I go for a different kind of guy I don't know but he never gives up."

"He's like that with everything" I said.

"What do you mean?"

"Like with soccer. You can be down 3 nothing with a minute to play and he's still like "Come on guys let's go" not like he thinks you can win or anything he just likes to keep trying."

"That's what he's like" Renee said.

"Yeah" I said.

"I'm just not interested in him."

"He's a great guy though" I said.

"I know" she said.

"Do you like that guy from um that other school? That you were telling your Uncle about?"

"I think so. We'll be away at different times over the summer I'm going away in June and the 2nd 1/2 of August and he's going away in July and the 1st 1/2 of August so we're never here at the same time we'll see next year though."

She said this like she was psyched like she was looking forward to next year and I know it sounds weird but until she said that I just never really realized next year was going to happen. Right after the summer. I mean I knew I'd be a Junior and everything and I thought about that but I just never really thought about it like that.

"We'll be Juniors" I said.

"Can you believe it?" said Renee.

The water was coming up on the beach and we were walking where it was coming pretty close to us but we stayed a few inches away from it you could hear people yelling down by the bonfire which was very far away and the wind was making a noise and it was dark but the moon was up there like a big light bulb. If she'd been my girlfriend and we'd been walking down the beach and holding hands on a night just like this I knew right then I'd be the happiest guy on planet Earth at that moment. I thought of holding her hand as friends but I didn't. We turned around and walked back.

When I came back Lenea was like "There's my date!" but she wasn't mad or anything she was just being funny. We all sat around. I had a 2nd brew but I wasn't drunk. My Dad lets me drink a beer at home with dinner if I want to so I'm used to it. A couple Senior guys we didn't really know came over and were all over the girls and hitting on them and they were pretty wasted and rude and I almost thought John was going to say something to them like "LISTEN man they're our dates" but he was mellow. They finally took off realizing they weren't going to get anywhere with our girls.

It was really late when I went to the bathroom inside. These 2 guys drinking drinks in the house were like "what's up man?" and I talked to them. Then I went to the bathroom and also looked around including going out on the balcony upstairs where I was the only 1 around and I could look down at the beach and see the bonfire and everyone. It was not as loud now and more mellow because it was really late. When I came back down and went outside on the beach Cindy and Pete were sitting there and I saw Randy and Wendy pretty close not exactly making out but hugging and kind of touching each other on this kind of plateau very close by where the sand went up a little and there was some grass and weeds in the sand. Lenea wasn't there and I went for a walk down the beach in the other direction from the 1 I went with Renee but much higher up so I wasn't by the water I was closer to where the plateau was and all the houses next to the beach.

I was walking along and a few couples passed me holding hands and with their arms around each other and 1 where the girl was holding the guy up so much it looked like he'd fall down if she moved. 1 group of guys went by and 1 of them saw me and yelled really loud "What's up Man???" and I was like "Hey" and I thought for a second they were going to jump me or something then the beach was pretty deserted and I looked up on the plateau and I saw something and I heard a noise that was definitely human like "Mmm Uuuh" or something and I slowed down and I saw these shapes sticking out of the grass and weeds on the plateau. They were 2 top 1/2s of people it was dark and they were moving around and sideways so I could only see the shapes and barely but somehow I knew it was John and Renee and it wasn't just her making noises either. He was going "Mmm uuh" too but in a totally different way. Like he was all over her. I wasn't walking anymore and I was pretty close to them even though I got there by accident but I could see they were just kissing and stuff they had no idea I was there they were totally in their own little world. They were sitting down and Johns arm I think was around her it was a little hard to tell whose arm was who because it was so dark. And I turned around and walked away casually because I didn't want them to hear me.

Back at the house Lenea was standing near the keg outside with a couple guys and a girl I went up and she put her arm around me and said in a friendly way "You keep disappearing."

"I was just on the beach" I said.

She introduced me to the people she was standing there with and I said hi. It was like way past the middle of the night now. Lenea said where is everybody and I said I don't know. I really like Lenea. She went inside and it was crazy in there the lights were off and people were all over each other on the couch and the stereo was blaring Pink Floyd which of course now I know every word of I thought about Caroline and how she would like it but she wouldn't be at Prom in about a mil-

lion years. Some people were very drunk but I didn't see anyone violent or puking I smelled pot in a few places. We sat
down in the kitchen at the kitchen table with 1 of the guys
from outside who was hitting on Lenea I could tell she wasn't
in to him though. Then we saw a spot on 1 of the couches and
we went over and sat down there the guy was talking a lot but
then I think he ran out of things to say because he finally shut
up. We all just kind of zoned out and sat there. Then Lenea
whispered to me "Will you come upstairs with me while I
smoke a cigarette I just want to get away from everyone."
"OK" I said. We got up (leaving the idiot there) and went up
the stairs. When we got up there we went back into that same
room and I closed the door because Lenea wanted to get away
from everyone and she sat down on the back of the bed with
her back leaning on the wall. I sat on the front of the bed
(which was sideways) not leaning on the wall to the side and
sort of in front of her. She had 2 cigarettes and some matches
and she lit up and started smoking.

"It's a nice party" she said.

"Yeah" I said. "Dinner was great too."

"I know" she said.

She smoked some more.

"Are you tired?" she said.

"No. Are you?"

"No."

Then she said "Here come sit here" and she sort of patted
the bed next to her but not like right next to her. I moved back
and sat with my back against the wall next to her.

"Do you mind the smoke?" she said.

"No" I said.

When she finished her cigarette she mushed it out on this empty plate somebody left there with some pizza crust on it. We just sat there for a while. We both had our feet down on the bed with our knees up and my knees went down to the side a little basically because of gravity and hers did too at the same time and they bumped into each other. Big deal. But then it happens twice more and then 1 time they don't go back up they stay touching. I'm like 'hmmmm'. I put my hand on my knee. A second later Lenea puts her hand on her knee. And then suddenly we're holding hands.

Then I said "Do you want a backrub?"

She said yes and we lay down and I rubbed her back. She had on a T-shirt that said Columbia where she wanted to go to school and eventually I went under it to rub. I could tell she was really into it because a couple times she went "Mmm" or "Ohhh". I was really into it because it feels good rubbing a persons back just because skin feels good. And also because doing something that feels good to another person (especially in a way that involves the senses) feels good.

What happened next is 2 peoples business so I'm not going to write about it. I know Mr. Rasfenjohn says write about everything you're thinking and feeling but what if he's wrong. I will say 1 thing though. When you feel (or might feel) strong feelings for someone you should express it verbally or physically (or both). This is part of nature. There is a strong connection between the body and the soul. When you feel this connection even just for a little while it's like everything is different now. You're more at 1 with the universe. You have felt the fullness of a womans flesh and it becomes a part of you then and forever and so does she. (Simultaneously it's like nothing is different at the same time. This is just a feeling it's hard to explain.)

Romantically my night with Lenea progressed to the end. Then we lay there for a long time. I could feel her breathing in and out and in and out.

Eventually she said "Let's go back down" and I said I'll be there in a minute. She went downstairs. It was a good time to think so I did. I thought about everything. Lenea and who she is and me. Should we be together? Did she like me? Probably. Renee. I felt a little weird almost like I cheated on her like she gives a fuck. But I was in love with her or was I? Maybe I wasn't. Maybe I just thought I was versus knowing it. Maybe I never really was in love with Renee. Maybe you can't be in love with somebody who isn't in love with you in the same exact way. Of course maybe Renee is secretly in love with me. Yeah right. To tell the truth in spite of many conversations I don't really know Renee that well for example in the way I know Lenea after sharing our dreams etc. with each other at dinner and fooling around. But also when I'm with or around Renee there's something very intense (maybe chemicals) just going on and I feel there is something special flowing between us. But I guess she flows that way with everybody. Life is complicated. People aren't who you think they are all the time because what do you know about what's really going on inside their mind. But on the other hand life is full of human beings who are often surprising. You never know what people will do and that can be good and interesting for example to keep the world full of surprises. So who knows. If you think about Douglas and not trusting people I think it's a bad idea. Because we are people. There's nothing wrong with that including mistakes by you or other people. Lies, deceit, arrogance, stupidity, sloth. These are bad but are in their own way a part of happiness, love, goodness, sex, and virtue. Get used to it.

I went downstairs. People were smoking and drinking and 1 couple was slow dancing in the living room I saw Lenea drinking a beer by the counter between the living room and the kitchen. I went over to her and she came over to me too and we stood there. She was drinking a beer and I had a couple sips. We shot the breeze a little. Cindy and her moron date appeared out of nowhere. Lenea leaned on me so her whole side was on me and she stayed like that while she talked to Cindy about nothing for a minute. Then the girls went off to talk more and I was standing there with Cindys date then he went to get more beer.

I went outside. The bonfire was still raging people had really kept it going. I stood there and looked at the water. Some people in their swim suits were swimming some of them were having chicken fights and screaming a lot. I saw the shapes of John and Randy in the water they both had girls I didn't know on their shoulders and their shirts off and they were running around and yelling and laughing and knocking each other and other people over then getting back up again and doing it again.

The after-Prom was almost over. Sophomore Year was a few hours from its final conclusion. Soon morning will appear and we will eat donuts and clean up. Soon we will get a ride on the chartered bus back to Hutch Falls because the limo was long gone. When we get dropped off at school the girls will cry and me and the guys will give each other Hi-5s and hug each other because it was a great year. Summer will officially begin. Summer a time for fun and reflection. Who knows what will happen. Then the cycle of life starts again.

But now this journey is drawing to a close. It was long and fruitful. I learned many lessons like be yourself and let your heart shine. And in the years to come I will experience life and friendship and always remember 10th Grade.

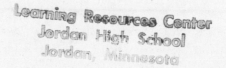